OTHER SHANE HINTONS

SHANE HINTON

BURROW PRESS | ORLANDO, FL

ALSO BY SHANE HINTON

Pinkies: stories

Radio Dark

We Can't Help It If We're From Florida (editor)

Book Design: Ryan Rivas
Published by Burrow Press. First printing.

ISBN: 978-1-941681-35-0
Library of Congress Control Number: 2025934580
Distribution by Asterism Books

Cover images: Nine puppets by Paul Klee
Dominique Uldry, Bern, CC BY-SA 4.0, via Wikimedia Commons

This project was supported by a University of Tampa Research
Innovation and Scholarly Excellence Award and an
International Faculty Development Grant.

A version of "Kingdom of the Wounded" was previously
published online by *Fence*.

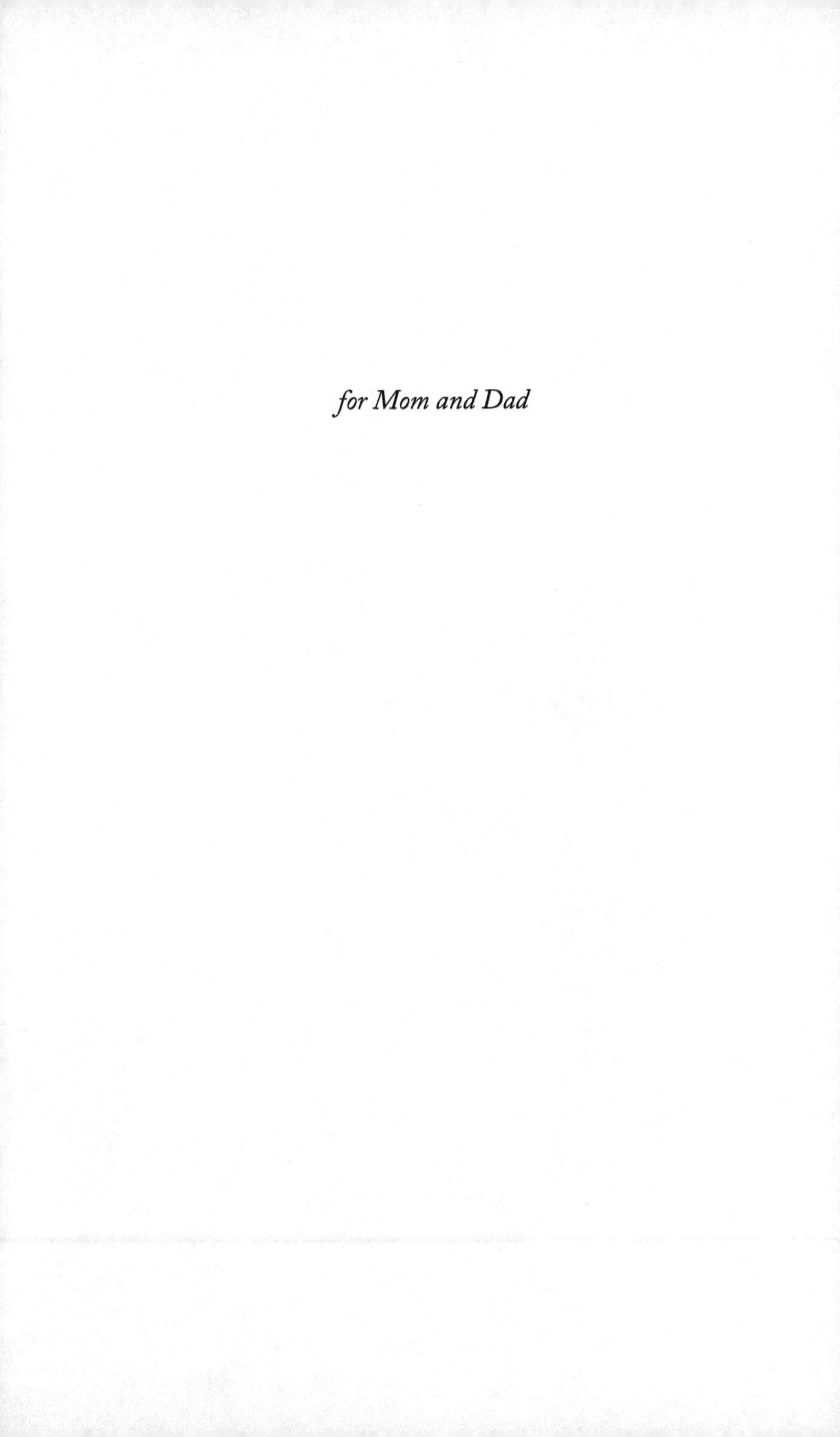

for Mom and Dad

CONTENTS

I was afraid to write this book, but the stories burrowed into me and erupted. If a medication could have killed them as larvae, I would have taken it.

I never wanted to lie to you.

ALL THAT IS BETWEEN MY HANDS

The attic stank of hot rodent urine, but we hung out up there because we liked tight spaces. Josie pulled the book of folklore from her backpack and we read together in the heat. Vibrant cartoon people populated the book's cover. One character sprinkled salt over their left shoulder, another nailed a horseshoe above a door frame. When Josie opened the book it made a sound like shedding skin. The pages were illustrated with black and white sketches. She turned to the section on witchcraft.

That scared me. We were only eight, but our preacher told us it was our duty to fight in the eternal war against Lucifer and his demons. The fate of our everlasting souls depended on our belief that Satan was waiting to ambush us behind every partially closed door. We had to remain vigilant, the preacher said, lest we be waylaid by his traps and machinations.

The book gave simple instructions on how to become a witch. You could inherit powers from your mother, if she was a witch. You could recite the Lord's prayer backwards seven times. You could bury the head of a black cat facing downward with a pea in its eye socket, then make a soup with the peas that grew from that plant. You could offer your life up to Satan in an irreversible pact that would damn your soul to hell for all eternity.

"We shouldn't even be looking at this," I said.

"We don't have time to grow a whole plant," Josie said.

Josie's mom dropped us off at my house every day after school. We were too young to stay home by ourselves, our parents reasoned, but between the two of us at least one would be able to dial the police, recite the emergency contact information my mom had taped to the wall above the phone on a curled piece of note paper. Our house was at the end of a long country road and there wasn't much trouble for us to get into.

We stood in the empty driveway with the book between us, a chunk of limestone holding it open. "Put one hand on your left foot and one hand on your head," Josie read. "Say three times, 'I give thee all that is between my hands.'" She looked up and smiled, her gray-blue eyes shining through her bangs. She didn't take our Bible lessons seriously, warnings about demons being at war for our souls, about this life being a trial. During church she drew obscene pictures in the margins of hymnals with the stubby pencils for writing names and amounts on tithe envelopes.

She lifted her left foot and grabbed it, so I did too. Neither of us wanted to be the first to speak. "On three," Josie said, and started counting while I tried to keep my balance.

The book said this pact could never be undone, but I knew God was inclined toward love and forgiveness, so I said the words the book told us to say, three times, hoping I could take it back with a little prayer and repentance. I believed the preacher and our Bible school teachers, who told us Satan and his demons were real, waiting for us right down the street, but I was more scared of the bullies on the baseball team who waited behind the dugout and punched me in the stomach while their parents laughed around the tailgates of their pickup trucks.

We finished the incantation and set our feet down, looking at each other expectantly. Josie held eye contact. She was beautiful. We had been each other's first dances at my uncle's wedding a few months prior. Our mothers had taken pictures and held their hands to their mouths as they watched. I didn't know what was supposed to happen when you became a witch. What I didn't understand then that I understand now is that people change in imperceptible ways, that our souls deplete so gradually we can't be conscious of the process.

It was early evening. My parents wouldn't be home from work for another hour or two. Josie raised her arm and let her fingers dangle toward the ground, like how my grandmother taught me to look for water with a dowsing rod, how old-timers dug wells wherever the point of a green twig pulled downward. Josie's fingers twitched and I wondered who we would hex, where we would fly under the full moon.

I heard a rustle of leaves and the soft crunch of tires in sand before a silver sedan with long scratches down its side rolled to a stop beside us. Josie smiled. A man in a stained undershirt stepped out of the car, his shoulder-length hair catching the breeze. He had a few days of gray stubble and his eyes were hidden behind large aviator sunglasses that sat crooked on his nose. "Daddy," Josie said, pressing her face into his belly.

I'd never met Josie's dad, but I knew he wasn't legally allowed to be around her anymore. As a baby he'd leave Josie in the crib so he could drink at the corner bar. One night Josie's mom came home early from her shift to find her alone, a stinking diaper leaking onto her favorite blanket. The court gave her mom full custody.

Josie's dad patted her on the back and held out his hand to me, like I was a peer. "You must be Shane," he said. I took his hand. It felt swollen. I wasn't supposed to let people come over when my parents were out. I looked at the door, thinking maybe I should call my mom at work. "Relax," Josie's dad said, "we don't need to tell anyone I was here. Certain people would not be very happy to hear that." He seemed to admire the fake-brick stucco exterior of our house, its decorative shutters, its lightly mildewed windows, before his eyes fell on the book, pressed flat on the ground by the chunk of limestone. "You got him to say it," he said, patting Josie on the head. "Who wants ice cream?"

Josie raised her hand and shook it in the air. I let mine come up a little bit, even though I was not supposed to leave the house for any reason when my parents were at work.

"Great," Josie's dad said. He turned toward the car, then stopped and turned back around. "I guess there's something we need to talk about first," he said. "You're not going to like this, Shane, but I don't want you to freak out." He paused and tilted his head as though waiting for me to object. "Here's the deal: I'm Satan." He smoothed down his gray hair and smiled wide, showing yellowed teeth. "I know, more handsome than you pictured. So you see what I mean. I need you to keep this quiet between us. Remember, you committed yourself to my service. 'All that is between my hands,' etcetera." He gestured at the book.

I followed Josie into the backseat and as we pulled away I looked at the fake brick front of my parents' house, at the little webbed balls caterpillars had built in the mortared cracks. They looked like nests, but in the past when I had pried them out with sticks and smashed them on the concrete nothing was inside.

Satan drove us to a gas station down the street and let us pick out whatever we wanted from an ice cream cooler with thick frost lining its interior. "On the house, right, Greg?" Satan said to the attendant, who just tilted his head forward a little instead of answering. We sat on a splintered wooden bench in front of the store. My ice cream was shaped like a cartoon rat with a brown chocolate head and two white gumballs more or less where you would expect eyes to be. "How's that ice cream?" Satan asked us. "You like those gumballs, Shane?"

I chewed one of the gumball eyes, enjoying the texture as my jaw worked on it.

"So," Satan said. "We need to talk about that Ms. Kludge."

Josie rolled her eyes. "She hates me." Red popsicle dye dripped down her chin.

Ms. Kludge was our Bible school teacher. She was a stickler about classroom conduct and had singled Josie out for sighing dramatically, saying it was disrespectful, that Josie was doing it on purpose, but it always seemed to me that Josie's sighs were unrelated to Ms. Kludge's lectures on Biblical creatures and family lineages. Ms. Kludge took everything personally.

"Josie has had detention every week for a month," Satan said. "She's got it in for our family. What do you guys say we pay her a visit?"

Josie licked the popsicle stick clean and jumped to her feet. I must have looked worried because Satan put his hand on my shoulder. "It's okay," he said. "Your parents won't be home for"—he closed his eyes like he was trying to remember something—"another forty-five minutes."

I got in the backseat of Satan's car, because what else could I do? I was a child. I wiped my sticky hands on the vinyl upholstery by my thighs. Satan caught my eyes in the rearview mirror. "Don't do that," he said. "I just had it cleaned."

We parked in a suburban neighborhood, in front of a house with a dead tree in the yard chopped into large chunks and stacked against an old chain-link fence. "Josie, I brought your tee-ball bat. You remember when they measured you at the sporting goods store? Remember how we picked out one that matched your height? I kept it even though your mom doesn't believe in organized sports," Satan said, shaking his head. "And I have my cordless drill."

Josie unbuckled her seat belt and threw her arms around her dad's neck from behind. "You're the best dad," she said, nuzzling her face into his long hair. He reached back awkwardly to touch her head.

"I've been surveying the neighborhood for a few days. With my evil powers, I mean." He pointed at the house next door. "Those neighbors are out of town on vacation." Then to the next house. "They don't get home until after dark."

What Satan was suggesting was very Old Testament. Most of my Biblical education had focused on the more brutal elements of the text: flaming swords of vengeance, plagues, boils, animal sacrifices. This seemed disproportionate, but he was a grownup. I had been taught to obey authority figures.

The grass by Ms. Kludge's front walkway was dying. She answered the door in a pink bath robe. "Shane? Josie? What are you doing here?"

Josie held the tee-ball bat against her leg. Satan kept the cordless drill behind his back.

Satan put a fake smile in his voice. "I'm Josie's dad," he said. "I'd like to speak with you about her performance in your class. Can we come in?"

Ms. Kludge looked older outside of the classroom, like a page from a book nailed to a tree trunk. "This is not when I usually hold parent conferences," she said, looking at Satan over the tops of her reading glasses. "You should schedule an appointment like everyone else."

"Please," Satan said. "I'm just a concerned parent."

Ms. Kludge shook her head and turned around. "Fine," she said. "But just for a minute. It's time for my evening devotional."

We followed Ms. Kludge's path between boxes overflowing with paperwork and cheap-looking As-Seen-On-TV products. She sat down in a recliner and motioned us toward the sofa. "Sit down," she said. The three of us squeezed onto the sofa. My thighs pressed against Josie's. Ms. Kludge crossed her hands in front of her face, steepling her fingers. "Josie is easily distracted and rude. These are symptoms of spiritual sickness. We cover important material in my class and she is unwilling to give it her full attention."

Satan cleared his throat and set the cordless drill down on the coffee table in front of him. Josie rested the tee-ball bat across her legs. Ms. Kludge looked at the drill, then the bat. "What did you say your name was?" she asked.

"Well, you're not going to like this," Satan said. "I'm the Devil. Lucifer. The Prince of Darkness. Belial. Beelzebub." He shrugged. Josie reached out and held his hand.

Ms. Kludge pursed her lips. "This is not funny," she said. "I see now where Josie gets it from."

Satan puffed out a sad-sounding exhale. "Look, you've got to stop giving my daughter so much detention," he said. "It's interfering with her extracurricular activities." He picked up the cordless drill and pulled the trigger. A small mechanical whir filled the quiet room.

Ms. Kludge stood. The bottom of her pink robe exposed her pale ankles. "Is this some kind of threat?"

"Sit down," Josie said.

Ms. Kludge looked again at the bat on Josie's knees, then at the drill in Satan's hand. She slumped into her recliner. "I won't compromise on classroom discipline," she said without conviction.

"Shane, do you want to take charge here?" Satan said. It was starting to get dark outside. From where we sat I could see into the pieces of tree piled against the fence, the rotten center of its trunk laid open. Satan held the cordless drill out to me. I wrapped my fingers around its handle, then pulled the trigger. My hand vibrated as the bit spun in front of my face.

I didn't want to hurt Ms. Kludge. She was no worse than Mr. Desmond, who had yelled at me for sleeping during class, or Ms. Sanders, who wrote me a referral for passing notes. Still, I had made a commitment to Satan, so when he nodded his head in Ms. Kludge's direction, I stood up and crossed the room.

My dad had taught me how to use a drill, to put my weight into it to get the bit started straight, so I pressed the metal against the top of Ms. Kludge's knee and leaned in.

She didn't move or try to get away. "Shane, your grades aren't even that bad," she said. "You still have time to get a B."

I didn't really care about my grades. Ms. Kludge didn't understand me at all.

The skin above her kneecap indented with my weight. I pulled the trigger and sprayed the walls with blood and pieces of meat before the bit settled into something hard and I knew I'd hit bone. Ms. Kludge screamed. Her head lurched toward the ceiling, but she kept her leg totally still. The drill was spinning freely now. My dad taught me how to recognize when the bit had pushed all the way through to the other side. Ms. Kludge howled out a prayer and I reversed the drill to back it out of her leg. Blood bubbled from a hole wide enough to accommodate a large metal bolt. Her mouth hung wide open but nothing came out.

Satan stood up from the couch. "That was good work," he said, patting me on the shoulder. "You're really doing my bidding here tonight. Right, I think that's settled. No more detention?"

Ms. Kludge nodded, drooling now. Blood pulsed out of her leg with each heartbeat, lapping over the edges of her wound.

The following Monday Ms. Kludge limped into class, a bulge beneath her skirt where her left knee was bandaged. She put her Bible on her desk but didn't open it like she usually did, didn't place the red silk bookmark carefully between the pages we'd be discussing that day. She lowered herself into her chair and took a deep breath. She opened a manila folder on the desk and said, "Shane, would you pass out these worksheets?"

She didn't make eye contact as I took the stack of paper. Her face was pale and sweat beaded at her hairline, just under the gray roots where her hair had grown out since she'd last dyed it. The worksheets were on Noah's ark, its dimensions, the animals on board, why certain creatures might have been left behind, where the boat might one day be discovered. Josie pushed the worksheet to the edge of her desk and looked out the window. Ms. Kludge kept her eyes cast down.

Not long after, Josie's mom lost her rental down the street from us and pulled Josie out of Bible school. That was the last I saw of her until I was thirteen. My mom loaded a white garbage bag full of clothes collected by women at the church into the backseat of her car and told me we were going to see Josie. The bag smelled like fabric softener and body odor. In front of a one-story apartment building, tenants sat smoking in sun-brittled plastic chairs, staring at us as we got out of the car. Josie's mom met us at the door. The apartment was tiny, just a single room. "I hate for you to see us like this," she said.

Josie stood up from the bed and led me outside while our moms sorted clothes on the dining table. I wanted to ask about her dad, because I had never seen him again and I couldn't tell if anything had ever come of my commitment to Satan. I thought I might have witchcraft powers, because sometimes bad things happened to the people I disliked. My P. E. coach got fired for making inappropriate calls to students. The kids who bullied me outside the dugout were plagued with acne and bad grades.

"Do you like it here?" I asked.

Josie shook her head and plucked something from my cheek. "You lost an eyelash," she said. My eyelashes were long. My mom's friends had started complimenting them, which made me realize I could see them all the time, at the top and bottom edges of my vision. Josie held up her finger, where a tiny black hair rested, curved like the blade of a scythe. "You have to make a wish when you lose an eyelash," she said, "then blow it off."

The neighbors leered at us from their plastic chairs. The air smelled like hot asphalt even though the sun was going down and the day was finally starting to cool.

I thought about it for a moment and wished that nothing would ever end, ever. Then I filled my lungs and blew.

STINKHORN

Rags the goat was ornery and unlikable. He had a hole in his head where he had knocked off one of his horns by ramming repeatedly against a fencepost. I could see his brain through the quarter-sized hole in his skull. My dad had to spray yellow antiseptic into the hole every few days. When Rags pissed he turned his head to catch the stream in his mouth. His long beard was permanently stained dark with urine. He wasn't a very good pet.

The day a racoon ate our chickens Rags just watched me sob, butting his head against the fence, impatient for me to put food in his bucket. I had been prepared for the chickens to die, on some level, because I had named them after the cartoon dinosaurs in one of my favorite movies. In the movie a meteor sent the earth into an animated ice age. The dinosaur family slowly starved to death onscreen.

"You stupid, stinking goat," I said. I was surrounded by the feathers and viscera of the chickens, my favorite pets. "I hope a beetle crawls into the hole in your head and needles your brain with its sharp legs."

Rags stomped his foot and lowered his head, but I wasn't afraid. He was only capable of blunt force and I had learned not to turn my back on him. I entered Rags' pen and threw a scoop of feed pellets in his bucket. I was bereaved at the loss of my chickens. I thought I closed the gate properly, nestling the hook into its eyelet, but I can't be sure.

At school my teacher showed us the Biblical evidence for dragons. "'I am a brother to dragons, and a companion to owls,'" she read, pointing to a page in our textbook with a picture of a green dragon breathing fire. "'Out of his mouth go burning lamps, out of his nostrils goes smoke. His breath kindles burning coals.' Haven't you all been told that dragons are make-believe, that they're just myths and legends? That was Satan, children, working to make you question the word of God, which is handily reprinted for you here in your textbook, colorfully illustrated to show you exactly what it describes. Don't listen to people who would diminish the word of God to metaphor. All we have is the text, which has survived fires and floods and purges for us to be able to hold it in our hands today. Who are we to question the word of the Lord our God? We are laying the foundation for His return, when the trumpet blasts will signal the coming of the savior, when the streets will run red with the blood of our unbeliever neighbors."

We didn't have many neighbors. There was only old Ms. Cardoso, whose children had died in the war. She lived by herself a few miles down the road. Her house smelled like spoiled milk. She had a picture of Jesus hanging crooked on the living room wall, his eyes lifted to the sky and his forehead bloody from the crown of thorns. It was painted on textured felt that looked itchy. Whenever we'd visit she sent us home with rice pudding that my mom always dumped in the trash. I wondered how much blood she could still have inside her, because she was small and withered. On the way home from school I'd watch her house go by from the window of the minivan. I hated to think that one day we'd be wading through what little was left of her blood.

We'd visited her that day, and after, when we pulled into our long driveway, lined with trees that were then just saplings but must now be thirty feet tall, my dad stood with the can of antiseptic spray at his side like a gunslinger with no one left to shoot. "Rags is gone," he said. The gate to the pen hung open. I tried to remember closing the latch, but couldn't. I had been distraught at the tragic death of the chickens. Maybe subconsciously I had wanted Rags to get out, wander into the road, get hit by a passing flatbed truck.

"You need to go find your goat," my dad said. He ran through the usual warnings: Don't go too close to the irrigation ponds. There's alligators in there and the sandy banks will crumble under your feet. Watch out for the tractors. Their moving parts will tear your limbs off and not even slow down. Stay away from the strawberry plants. They're covered in herbicides and pesticides and will damage your organs. "And take off your school shoes," he said. "The farm is not the place for school shoes."

I nodded and handed my mom the repurposed whipped cream container of rice pudding that Ms. Cardoso had sent home with us. The once-white plastic lid was stained orange. I took off my shoes and put my socks inside them.

My dad put his hand on my shoulder. "Your school shoes were very expensive," he said. "I'll take them inside for you."

I searched the sandy ground for tracks, but saw only the imprints of tractor tires, great looping patterns that overlaid each other between the rows of strawberries. I tried to stay out of the clouds of poison sprayed by the tractors, but a toxic metal taste settled on my tongue. After a long while, emerging from a drainage ditch, I found hoofprints leading toward an unused barn at the edge of the property.

My uncle, a tall man with leathered skin, had told me to stay out of the old barn. The roof was coming apart. It was full of rusting equipment and half-empty barrels of chemicals. I stood at the wide door, looking into the darkness. I could hear the faint jingling of Rags' collar. I said a quiet prayer for safety and stepped inside. The dark room spread out in front of me. I could barely see him on the far side of the barn, a white shape almost wholly obscured by shadows.

"Rags," I said. "I'm sorry for what I said about your brain. I was sad about the chickens. Please come home."

He didn't move. I stepped closer, slowly, into the darkness. A few steps in and I couldn't see the ground clearly, but I kept my eyes on Rags, afraid to lose sight of him if I looked away. The concrete floor was rough and cold against my feet. I could hear Rags slowly crunching on something. I imagined him watching me step ever closer, his sharp mean little teeth churning whatever it was he'd found. "Stop eating that," I called out. I thought about turning back, afraid of the snakes that were surely coiled among decaying engine parts, but when I looked at the door it was so much farther away than I expected. I took a breath and stepped directly onto a roofing nail. The nail went so deep into my foot it hit bone. Pain shot all the way up my leg. I collapsed on the concrete and touched the wide base of the nail, flush with my skin. I cried out to God and whoever would listen. The diesel engines of the tractors roared in the distance, the sound growing and fading as they moved up and down the rows.

"Rags," I said, begging now, even though the goat and I never had a close relationship. "Please."

Rags didn't move. I crawled toward him, sweeping my hands in front of me, feeling for other nails that might have fallen from the roof. When I got closer I could feel shards of glass at Rags' feet. He was eating them, crunching them between his teeth, dropping his head to pick up more. I took him by the collar and rose on one foot. "I'm glad you didn't get hit by a truck," I said. "That was a mean thing to want." Leaning on him for support, my fingers tangled in his rough fur, I led Rags out of the barn, slow and steady, then home through the strawberry fields.

My mom put me on the kitchen counter and extracted the rusty nail from my foot. She washed the wound out with stinging dish soap over and over, until she was satisfied I wouldn't get lockjaw. She was always worried back then that something was going to give me lockjaw.

The glass had cut up Rags' belly and he was dead by sundown. My dad carried him across the pasture behind our house and buried him at the edge of the pine trees. When I cried over him in class my teacher told me that animals have eternal souls, even goats that drank their own piss and had holes in their heads so big anyone nearby could see the soft pink folds of their brains. Over the next few weeks, a purple and orange mushroom that smelled like rotting meat grew over Rags' grave, and when I visited I could hardly stand the smell. Still, I made myself sit there with the mosquitoes biting my arms and neck, because it was my fault he was dead.

It was a full moon the night Rags came back as a ghost. I was looking out my bedroom window at the pasture in front of our house when I saw him standing by the oak tree. Without him and the chickens the yard had felt abandoned. I even missed him a little bit, the way he'd let me touch his ribcage if he was in a decent mood. So I was happy to see him there, shimmering the way they always tell you ghosts shimmer, like they'll dissipate if you try to hug them. He moved across the yard and slowly stood on his hind legs, placing his front hooves on the windowsill until we were face to face through the glass.

"Shane," he said. "It's good to see you. I'm sorry I was not a very good pet."

"I'm sorry too," I said. "I think I left your pen open. I wanted you to run away."

He chewed thoughtfully on something I couldn't see. His yellow eyes locked on mine. "It was just a little mistake," he said. "Don't be too hard on yourself."

I started to cry. I hadn't been able to tell anyone about the gate, though I'm sure my parents suspected it was my fault. "That's nice of you to say, Rags."

"I don't know why I ate that glass," he said. "It didn't even taste good. It cut my mouth up."

"They always say that about goats, how they'll eat anything."

"That's offensive, but, you know, true to an extent, I guess," Rags said. He didn't look upset with me.

"Will you stay out there tonight?" I asked. I hated full moons. I could see all the way across the pasture to the hard road. I felt sure one day I would see a shadowy figure walking slowly across the open field, making its way toward our house, and I didn't know what I would do when that day came.

"Sure," Rags said. "I don't have anything else to do." He backed away from the windowsill and turned to face the pasture, his jaw slowly working whatever it was he'd found to chew in death.

From then on he followed me wherever I went. Through the parking lot at the grocery store, for instance, or on the playground at school. No one else could see him. I sat by myself a lot, making sure we were alone so I could talk to him. We carried on great conversations. He told me about the structure of his stomach, describing each of the four chambers in detail, pausing to let me ask questions, never talking over me.

Outside on the playground, a kid with curly hair and a perpetually runny nose pegged me on the side of the head with a dodgeball. "You're out," the snotty kid said. I couldn't argue with him. That was how the game was played. I walked off past the sidelines and sat on a fence far away from the other kids. Rags was beside me. I watched as a girl went so high on a swing I was sure she was going to circle all the way around like so many of us had dreamed of. She reached the apex of her swing and fell straight down until the chains jerked tight.

"I think one day she'll make it," I said.

"There are rules," Rags said. "I don't think it's possible."

Rags and I looked at each other. The hole in his head didn't seem nearly as gross as it had in life.

"Why don't you have any friends?"

"I have friends," I said, but looking out across the playground I couldn't point to anyone who would have considered me a friend. "These people are all my friends."

"That's not what friendship is," Rags said.

"You're my friend."

He nodded and started chewing.

After recess, Rags watched through the classroom window as our teacher told us about the coming Armageddon. Major points of her lecture included the mark of the beast and what forms it might take, the appearance of plagues and pestilences and false idols. "We must not overlook the signs," she said. "Sometimes those signs are numerical. Sometimes they are just intuitive thoughts. We must not question God's design for us, above all, and we must act with certainty when we receive His messages. If we are confused, that is a shortcoming, a flaw in our spiritual armor. We must always be convinced. To doubt is to invite the influence of Satan."

Rags floated beside the minivan on the way home from school. I sat in the back seat so I could talk to him through a window that only opened a sliver. "Do you think Ms. Cardoso is going to Hell?" I asked as we passed her house. I could see her driveway through Rags' translucent body. He turned to look at her old wooden house, at the trees and shrubs overgrown and pressing up against it.

"There's no way to be sure," he said.

My mom looked at me in the rearview mirror. "Shane," she said, "your teachers say you don't have any friends."

"Everyone is my friend," I said.

"That's not what friendship is," my mom said. She gripped the steering wheel until her knuckles turned white. "Kids need friends. Your dad found something for you today. I think you're going to like it."

At our house a black and white dog was tied by its neck to a fence post. My dad stood beside it, smiling, hands on his hips. "Look who wandered up to the house today," he said. "Every kid needs a dog."

My mom had never let us have dogs because she had been traumatized by one when she was a kid, knocked to the ground and bitten. She stood behind me as I approached the black and white dog. I could feel the bruise of her anxiety at the base of my neck.

The dog was skinny and missing patches of hair. It pulled against the rope tied around its neck. Rags stood beside it, silent, appraising.

"This dog has fleas," Rags said.

I didn't know if I was ready to love another animal, but I didn't want to break my parents' hearts with anything less than enthusiasm. I looked back at them. My dad was proud. My mom wrung her hands together.

"I can see its bones," she said. "Is it sick?"

My dad shrugged. "I think I've got some flea medicine around here somewhere. That skin looks itchy."

"Thank you so much," I said. "This dog will be my best friend."

The dog was not used to being constrained. He kept pulling at the rope, letting it dig into his neck until he choked and coughed. "Stop it," I told him. "You're being ungrateful."

My dad put his arm around my mom's shoulder and turned her toward the house. "Don't let him bite you," my mom said. I nodded.

I sat with Rags just outside where the dog could reach. Rags looked distracted, chewing again. When my parents were far enough away I asked Rags what he was eating.

He opened his mouth to show me. On his ghost tongue shards of glass caught the late afternoon sunlight. The dog looked at where Rags was sitting and started pulling against the rope again, shaking his head back and forth, trying to squeeze out of the collar my dad had tightened around his neck.

Rags went over to the bowl my parents had set out for the dog. Inside, flies crawled over chicken bones from our dinner a few days earlier. "Dogs are supposed to be good pets," he said, "but they whine too much."

The dog pulled away from me when I tried to inch closer. "I don't want any more pets," I said.

Rags nodded. "It's really a question of who owns whom."

The dog started chewing on the rope, and I could tell he would be able to get through it if he committed. He'd probably wandered up to our house looking for food, and now he was caught. People used to dump dogs they didn't want out on our country road all the time. Usually my dad would shoot them with a BB gun and stomp his feet until they ran off. There weren't many places for the dogs to go back then, before developers bought up the land and turned it all into suburban neighborhoods for people moving down from up north, tired of shoveling snow and having their cars rust prematurely from the salted roads, not realizing that down here things rust prematurely due to the saltwater in the air, that no matter how quickly or slowly you expect things to decay they always do it faster than you think they should.

THE DEVIL'S DITCH

The Devil's Ditch was the only place in our redneck town where we could get up some decent speed on our skateboards. The concrete embankment hugged the side of a hill that sloped toward a creek and ended up under a bridge. The Ditch was built to catch runoff from the surrounding neighborhoods, which had been orange groves before disease killed them off. Rumor was the church at the top of the hill was Satanic because of the weird messages on the signboard, and because a line of silver meat hooks hung from the trees behind the building.

Charleston slammed the nose of his skateboard down and I dropped in behind him. That summer Charleston led and I followed. I tried to copy the way his knees bent, the way his fingers grazed the tops of the concrete walls as he carved. Where he flowed, I wobbled. When he popped a little ollie at the top of a wall, I tried to do the same, but when my feet came down the board shot out in front of me. My skull bounced off the ground. I lay still for a while and let the heat radiate up through the concrete into my back. The Ditch was scattered with broken glass and rusted screws washed down from construction sites. From the ground I could see the debris clearly, raised aberrations on the surface of the concrete.

I sat up, dizzy. At the bottom of the hill the creek bubbled past. My board had landed a few feet from the water. Charleston brought it over and sat down beside me.

"Do you feel any different?" Charleston asked. "Are you seeing energy auras around things? Sometimes a head injury will allow you a glimpse through the veil."

I touched the back of my head. No blood, but already a knot. "No," I said, but when I looked up at the guard rail on the bridge, silver in the light of the afternoon sun, a deep green patch burned into my vision. I looked away and everything else had a damaged hue. Sometimes people in the grip of a terminal illness or major life event are able to see the face of God. We learned this in church. The page in our Sunday school textbook showed a picture of a man in a blue suit and striped tie, staring upward with his mouth hanging open. I shook my head. My brain felt like it was rattling around. Cars passed by on the bridge. "Just looks like traffic," I said.

As we walked back up the hill Charleston noticed the smell. "Seared meat?" He wrinkled his nose.

At first I thought he was talking about the phantom scents that preceded an outburst of prophecy or seizure, but he pointed toward the top of the hill and raised his eyebrows. We were always on the lookout for a free meal. We stashed our boards in the tall grass and followed the smell of smoke to where the old church sat back from the road. It had a steeple with slatted boards and peeling white paint. The parking lot was unpaved. Tire tracks charted where the grass had been depressed by the congregation. The signboard by the road stated FLESH GIVES BIRTH TO FLESH in black block letters.

At the back of the church, an industrial-sized smoker was set up on a concrete pad. The kind that tows behind a truck, big enough to feed a large party or a small group of believers. I lifted the lid of the smoker and six turkeys were lined up on the grate inside, each wrapped in mesh netting.

"Do Satanists eat meat?" I asked.

"Maybe," Charleston said, shrugging. "I think it depends on what kind of meat, and what time of the month it is?"

We'd been told a lot of things about Satanists by sweaty preachers, things we suspected might not be true but had been taught not to doubt.

I don't think I meant to steal the turkey. Between the head injury and the heat I was feeling like a character in a cautionary tale. I reached out to touch the skin, red and brown and flecked with pepper, but my fingers dug deeper into the meat than I intended. Charleston smiled at me. I lifted the turkey from the smoker and we took off running toward the bridge at the bottom of the hill.

The turkey was slick and heavy. It kept wanting to slip away. Charleston ran in front, jumping over stinging nettle plants, his thin legs wire-framed against the sky. The turkey thudded against my chest as I tried to keep up. When we reached the shadow of the bridge I plopped the turkey on the concrete between us.

"I hope no one saw," Charleston said. He wrenched and pulled and finally peeled the wet pink netting from the skin of the bird, leaving a grid of indentations behind.

"I think the Satanists would have encouraged us to steal from them," I said. I twisted and yanked at a turkey leg, trying to pop it free from carcass. When it wouldn't come loose I lifted the whole bird to my mouth. As soon as I bit into it, I could tell it wasn't right. The meat squished between my teeth. It tasted sulfurous.

"I think this turkey was sick," I said. "Why would they cook a sick turkey?"

Charleston dug his finger into the hole where I'd bitten and pulled out a chunk of stringy meat. He laughed. "It's still raw."

I bared my teeth to show the gray meat tangled up in them, partially smiling, partially grimacing. Charleston fake-heaved. My stomach rumbled. I wanted to swallow the meat. It smelled delicious but tasted rank. I spit it into the dirt.

Below us, the creek was so low I could see the sandy bottom through the sweet-tea colored water. It was only the beginning of the rainy season and there were still white islands in the middle of the stream. I stood and lifted the turkey over my head. "We are gathered here on the bank of this river to witness a transformation," I said, parroting what I'd heard the preacher say before baptismal ceremonies at the local public pool. "We have known this bird only a short while, but we pray that what enters this water condemned by sin may emerge washed clean in the eyes of God."

The turkey was heavy. My arms started to shake. Hot grease ran down my forearms and gathered in the hollow of my collarbone. The edges of my sight blackened a little, then came back into focus.

"The creek is full of pesticides," Charleston said. His jaw was tight.

"I baptize this bird in the name of the Father, and the Son, and the Holy Ghost." I threw the turkey as hard as I could. It hit the bank and started rolling, gathering seeds and sand spurs, before splashing into the shallow water and bobbing to the surface. I watched it float slowly toward the center of the creek. Charleston reached up and held one of my still-raised hands. A membrane of turkey grease slicked our palms.

CHARLESTON'S STEPDAD, ALFIE, WAS IN THE SHADE OF A wide oak tree working on his pickup truck when we walked into the yard. The engine compartment swallowed his oil-stained forearms. "Lord, please loosen this nut," he grunted. "Free it from the bondage of rust and let it turn as you surely intended, having given it threads to follow and a shape to fit this wrench." His body was taut. Then, with a tiny squeak, the nut came free and he relaxed. "Where have you two been?" He straightened up and put a hand at the small of his back. He set his wrench down on the bumper and picked up a beer.

Charleston held up his skateboard. Alfie shook his head, then drained the beer and threw the empty can to the ground. Alfie was shorter than Charleston by more than half a foot. He had the guitar-string muscles of manual labor in his arms and legs, but a round belly that sagged against his t-shirt. "What a waste of a beautiful day," he said, then opened another beer and leaned back into the truck. "Lord, please give these young men some direction."

Charleston started up the stairs to the porch.

"You know what? Come back here," Alfie said, "I want to teach you two something."

Charleston dropped his skateboard upside down on the porch. One wheel spun slowly.

"Hold this." Alfie handed Charleston the wrench. "See there?" He pointed to a rusted bolt. "Give it a twist."

Charleston leaned in and locked the wrench onto the nut, then pulled, the muscles in his arms straining. "Pull," Alfie said. "Come on, now. Put your weight behind it." Charleston leaned back, not looking up from the dark cavity at the front of the truck. Alfie smiled and lit a cigarette. "Come on, boy, you can do it." Charleston gave one more heavy tug and let go of the wrench. "Just kidding," Alfie said. "I knew you couldn't do it." He laughed and spit in the dirt, then blew smoke in Charleston's face. Charleston looked away, blinking, clenching his fists at his sides.

"Now you," Alfie said, handing me a spray can. "Give it a little squirt." I stepped up to the hood of the truck and leaned in, trying not to cut myself on the rusted metal. "Go on," Alfie said, nudging me in the kidney with his pointer finger.

I held down the red plastic nozzle and coated the nut in spray. "All right, easy now," Alfie said. "That stuff's expensive. Your job here is done. You're up, my prodigal stepson. Show me what you can do."

Charleston and I traded places again and Alfie began to pray. "Lord, please let this silicone-based lubricant penetrate the outer layer of rust that you have so righteously crafted around this nut, Lord, and please give my stepson strength in his forearms and biceps sufficient to turn that nut, Lord, so that I may get this truck running once again, so that I don't have to ride to work with Trevor anymore, Lord, because as you know, Trevor won't let me smoke in his new truck, Lord, which you allocated to him in his father's will, meanwhile leaving me here to struggle with this old Chevrolet, which is for some reason part of your plan, Lord, even if your humble servant does sometimes wish your plan included a bit more material prosperity, Lord, in the form of a reliable mode of transportation."

Charleston looked over his shoulder at Alfie, and Alfie slapped him on the back of the head, not too hard, but hard enough. "Well, go on, boy."

Charleston pulled hard on the wrench and I thought it wasn't going to work. Alfie lifted his arms and his face to the sky, his open beer in one hand and his cigarette in the other. "Lord, please give this stepson of mine the heft, Lord, the spirit, to break this nut free." Charleston's arm jerked backward as the nut broke free. "Amen," he exclaimed, spilling a little bit of beer on his shirt. "My boy," he said. "What did I tell you? Thank you, Jesus. I've been working on that all day."

Alfie tilted the silver beer can and dripped the remaining liquid into his mouth. He crushed the can in the middle and threw it into the overgrown hedges lining the porch, then followed us in through the screen door, letting it bang shut behind him.

"Just taught these boys a thing or two about faith and auto maintenance," Alfie said to Charleston's mom, Rosette. He sat down on the couch atop a blue knitted blanket with the logo of the university from just up the interstate stitched into the center. He never graduated from high school, but spent every Saturday watching college football, rooting for this university where he'd dreamed of playing.

Rosette was reading a paperback featuring a picture of a man in a half-buttoned shirt on the cover. She licked her finger and turned the page without looking up. "I hope you already ate," she said. In the corner of the room an oscillating fan turned slowly back and forth. When the fan pointed at Rosette it blew hair into her eyes and she stuck out her lower lip to blow it back to her forehead. The hem of her oversized floral dress fluttered in the breeze, exposing her blue-veined calves.

Charleston dug around in the kitchen for a can of shredded chicken breast and heated it up in a skillet while I picked at congealed spaghetti sauce on the table with a dirty fingernail. He sprinkled the chicken with powdered parmesan cheese and served it on colorful paper plates left over from a birthday party. I waited for Charleston to sit down, then started eating the canned chicken slowly, chewing each bite longer than I needed to. Charleston closed his eyes every time he put a forkful into his mouth.

Alfie slapped the remote control against his palm. "Just give these batteries enough juice, Lord, to let me turn on this game and set the volume to an appropriate level for college sports, Lord, which is to say loud, to simulate the noise of the students, Lord, cheering on their boys." He slapped the remote against his palm again. "These boys, Lord, who are soldiers in your service, out on the field of life demonstrating the fine physical capabilities you've seen fit to grant them, the wavering musculature underneath their mesh shirts, Lord, rippling in the heat." The TV came to life at full volume. The cheers of the crowd sounded like static noise. "All glory to you, God," Alfie said. "I trust that you will give these young men strength to crush the opposing team, because, as you are no doubt aware, Lord, my blood pressure is already high."

Rosette sighed and thumped her hand on the table beside her. "I can't think with you praying like that," she said, waving her paperback at Alfie. "I'm just getting to the good part. This poor woman is about to get all the kisses she ever wanted. She's walked through great personal tragedy and unimaginable pain." Alfie waved his hand dismissively and pulled a beer from a small cooler at his feet. He wiped the rim of the can with the knitted blanket and then cracked it open, took a long drink, and belched.

"Disgusting," she said. "I don't even know why I married you."

Alfie looked up and smiled. He was missing an incisor on the left side of his mouth and he flicked his tongue into the hole where it used to be, filling the space with pink flesh. "Yes you do," he said, and Rosette giggled.

"You're so nasty," she said, smiling over the top of her book.

Charleston stood and tossed our plates in the trash. "Let's go upstairs," he said.

"Next time wait for a commercial," Alfie said as we crossed in front of the TV. "I could have missed some important play calling. Lord, forgive these boys, as they know not how thoroughly they disrupt my enjoyment of the game."

Charleston's room was an unplanned addition, a converted attic where bent nail heads studded bare plywood walls. It was poorly insulated and the window-mounted air conditioner could only struggle against the humidity. Alfie built the stairs and the walls of Charleston's bedroom using scraps from a jobsite that he was supposed to take to the county dump.

Charleston plugged in the air conditioner. Even as the room cooled we kept sweating, leaving outlines of ourselves on the mattress where we sat. We played a video game on an old TV, passing the controller back and forth each time the character onscreen fell off his skateboard and into the pixelated sea in the background. My head still ached. The bump at the back of my skull was swollen to the size of a baby's fist.

"I wish they'd knock this place down," Charleston said, handing me the controller. Everything around his house had already been bulldozed. New neighborhoods were going up anywhere they could fit. There were construction sites all over town. Men in bright orange vests moved dirt and pushed over trees. I couldn't recognize places that had once been familiar. "I wonder where all of these people are coming from."

"The weather is good for old people's lungs," I said. My grandfather had died of tuberculosis and my mom told me about the sound of his coughing. No one was allowed to hug him.

"That's just what people used to think before they understood medicine," Charleston said.

My video game character hit a snake and slid across the screen on his face. Lightning bolts of pain appeared above his head. I handed the controller back to Charleston.

"I don't think there's any space left," Charleston said, and put his tongue against his upper lip in concentration, moving the controller in time with the character onscreen.

Droplets of spit reflected the blue light from the TV. "They're scraping the topsoil off. That's the best part of the soil." The words GAME OVER flashed on the screen and he hammered the start button until the blinking sound of a coin chimed through the speakers.

Alfie whooped downstairs. Rosette laughed. We could hear everything through the floor as clearly as if we were sitting next to them. "That's it, boys," he said. "Get in there and show them how it's done. Make them take it. Right up the middle. Lord, please make a hole in this defense wide enough for me to drive that old Chevrolet through, once I get it running. Lord, give the opposing team's coach diarrhea, Lord, right here in the middle of the game. Let him run off the field at halftime clutching his belly like it's about to spill out onto your sacred gridiron, Lord, like he's going to lose it on TV in front of all these students and their proud parents, Lord, and the administrators of our great state institution, and the folks in the cheap seats, and the fans at home like me, Lord, because tomorrow is church, Lord, and we couldn't make the drive to and from the stadium with all we've been drinking, Lord, even if we did have a functioning pickup truck."

It was starting to get cool in Charleston's room, so I lay down on the mattress and rolled on my side. I closed my eyes and listened to Charleston clack the buttons on the controller. I could still picture the masked character sliding on a handrail and jumping over crumbling portions of the highway. There wasn't traffic in the video game, so the digital skater had the street to himself. I fell asleep thinking of the way my feet would vibrate if I tried to skate down the decaying street out front of Charleston's house, how my wheels would bounce over the pebbles in the asphalt, how any little pothole would throw me face-first to the pavement.

I WOKE UP WITH DRIED SWEAT ON MY SKIN. BESIDE ME, Charleston's breathing was slow and regular like he was asleep, but his eyes were open and staring up at the plywood ceiling. I tried to be still, to pretend I was asleep, but he rolled on his side to look at me. For a minute our breathing was synchronized, our chests rising and falling in time, then he pulled back the covers and went downstairs. The moon was in the window over the tops of the oak trees outside. When Charleston opened the door at the base of the stairs Alfie spoke up. I held my breath.

"They lost," he said, in the lilting voice of an all-day drunk, like he was on the verge of tears. "I never made it to college, never made it through high school, even. Got caught smoking a joint under the bleachers and boom, expelled."

"That's disproportionate," Charleston said.

"I bet you think it's all disproportionate," Alfie slurred. "Everything in this world is out of whack? You going to figure it all out? You think you're so cute, think you're getting away with every little thing? You think I don't know what goes on up there in that room I built for you with my own two hands? You think I'm too stupid to figure it out?" His voice was rising now, the words ran together, gathering speed.

"You could have put in more insulation," Charleston said, his voice rising to match Alfie's.

"Don't you tell me how to insulate my own house," Alfie said. "I pay the bills around here. What have you ever done? Cook your little dinners? We can eat just fine out of the frozen foods aisle. Did you ever think about that? I work in the heat all day, boy. I don't spend my time in a nice air-conditioned classroom, book-learning. Christ. Think of the electricity bills."

A loud banging rattled the AC unit. The sounds of heavy contact, muffled grunts. Something hit the wood floor hard enough to shake the house, then the screen door slapped shut. I got up from bed and looked out into the yard. Alfie was doubled over, hands on his knees. The moon was bright but he was in the shadow of the oak tree.

"You're going to miss me," he shouted. "I'm the only one who ever taught you how to replace a spark plug. You wouldn't even know what a spark plug is if it wasn't for me. Don't you forget it."

I heard Rosette's door open and she emerged on the front porch. "Come on to bed, Alfie. It's past midnight. You don't want to throw a tantrum on the Lord's day, do you? Don't you think he's going to frown on that? Isn't that what Pastor Jimmy told us? The Lord frowns upon those that throw tantrums on His day?"

Alfie seemed to have caught his breath. He stood up straight and rolled his shoulders back, then turned and walked up the driveway. Rosette shook her head and went back inside. "Real nice," she said, in the living room to Charleston. "Just real, real nice. You know his team lost. What are you trying to do around here? Throw everything into chaos? Don't you think we have enough of that already?"

"It's not my fault they've got a poorly coached team," Charleston said.

"You've just got it all figured out," Rosette said. "Let's just turn all our problems over to Charleston. Mr. Big Brain. Mr. Can't Get His Mom Something Decent For Mother's Day."

Charleston's steps back up the stairs were slow but light. He'd learned to climb them in near silence. He lay down in bed and I rolled over to look at him. The light from the window was dim but I could see that his lip was split open. I traced the wound with the tip of my pointer finger.

THE NEXT MORNING ROSETTE PACED BACK AND FORTH IN the living room, her stomach and breasts heaving as she worked herself up. "I figured he'd sleep it off in the woods," she said. "Check again."

Charleston leaned over the back of the sofa and held the curtains open, making a show of turning his head back and forth slowly. We were both wearing polo shirts and slacks for church. Rosette liked to make the early service because she felt it was more Godly to wake up early and because there were more doughnuts than at the late service.

"All right," she said. "Let's just go, I guess."

The backseat of Rosette's minivan was covered with cigarette burns from where embers she and Alfie flicked out the window had blown back in and smoldered unnoticed into the upholstery. I stuck my finger into one of the holes between my legs and picked at its cauterized edges, prying out little pieces of yellow foam.

At church Rosette loaded up a small paper plate with

powdered doughnut holes and we took a seat in the back. "Sit on your hands," Rosette said, swatting my arm to stop me from flipping through a hymnal. Charleston looked upward, over the congregation. I followed his stare to a stained-glass depiction of a man sprawled against a rock and bleeding from the head.

The central message of the service was about being delivered from one thing and into another, about how no one can anticipate the nature of God's plan for us, how it would be presumptuous to think that anything we might want would be what God wants for us, how it's our job to let go of old habits, old cell phone plans that were costing too much money, old life insurance policies with high monthly premiums based on our many pre-existing conditions. "God won't cut those things out of your life for you," the pastor said, mopping his neckline with a black and white paisley handkerchief, "but he can give you the scissors. Well, he can't really give them to you, but he can show you where to get a good discount."

Someone shouted, "Amen!" The pastor raised his sweat-stained handkerchief in appreciation.

After the service we sat in silence around the dining table with a red and white striped bucket of chicken between us, passing a foam container of macaroni and cheese in a circle. "This stuff is made in huge vats," I said. "It comes in bags, then they just drop the whole bag into some hot water and it tastes better than homemade."

"What's wrong with you?" Rosette snapped. She still had powdered sugar on the front of her dress and it looked like the flowers on her chest were coated with frost. "Can't you see I'm in mourning? What kind of a thing is that to tell someone anyway? Plastic bags? Do you think I want to hear that?"

We chewed for a while in silence, our jaws working, our tongues squirming to pick little bits of meat from between our teeth. I took the smaller pieces and gnawed on the cartilage between the bones.

AT FIRST THE KNOCK SOUNDED LIKE IT MIGHT BE A BRANCH whacking against the side of the house. Each thump was followed by a wet sucking sound.

"Oh God," Rosette said. "It's those kids egging the house again. Here in the hour of my greatest sorrow."

Charleston and I ran to the door. I looked over his shoulder, not wanting to fight, but ready to act like I would. Nobody was there. I stood on my toes, hands clenched at my sides. Though I'd never thrown a punch, I had been hit a few times, and my jaw tingled in anticipation. Charleston flung open the door. The turkey I'd tossed into the creek stood in the doorway, unnaturally, on the visible bone stumps of its legs. Charleston moved aside and held his hand over his mouth. The bird waddled into the living room and stood in a ray of midday sun. Its skin, red and brown when we had stolen it from the smoker, was washed out white and gray. It was rotten, decomposed by the combination of being barely cooked and submerged in runoff from farms and construction sites. It dripped a large stain onto the carpet. The smell of late-stage decay followed it. I swallowed a mouthful of partially digested macaroni and cheese puke.

Rosette pushed her chair back and stood up. "Alfie? Is that you? Give us a sign. Oh, Lord, is this Alfie? Have you taken him from us and sent him back in the form of partially smoked meat?"

"That's not how reincarnation works, Mom," Charleston said, burping a little through his fingers.

The bird turned back and forth like it was surveying the room, then waddled slowly to the couch, sat down in Alfie's ass groove, and pressed its spine against the university blanket. The bird started doing something with its wing, twisting it forward, like it was stretching out a kink, extending the joints until the featherless tip pointed out across the room to the TV. Rosette held a cigarette between her fingers, her eyes wide.

"Mom," Charleston said. He held out a hand to stop her, but she was already moving across the room. She turned on the TV and college football highlights came on, the announcers giving a breakdown of the next weekend's most anticipated matchups. The bird relaxed its wing, letting it fold against its side, and seemed to exhale as it leaned into the cushions.

Rosette knelt by the couch, reaching out her hand to touch the turkey's breast, its skin sticking to her fingers and pulling slightly away from the meat with each caress. "What happened, Alfie? Did you fall in the creek and drown? Were you abducted by gang members? Did they drive you out into the swamp and tie you to a tree and let the alligators finish you off? Oh God," she sobbed, "that's it, isn't it? You were a victim of gang violence." She snuggled her face between the turkey's wing and its chest.

On the TV, commentators reviewed the previous night's loss. "These guys were really out for vengeance," one said over a clip of a player being vaulted into the air and spun in slow motion, coming down hard on his neck. "This is more than a rivalry. What we saw last night was out-and-out hatred. I don't even know how they clean the bloodstains off the field after a night like that, do you, Gary?"

"Pressure washing, maybe," the other commentator said. "Bleach? There's something that's supposed to get blood out, but it's not what you'd expect. Vinegar?"

"Baking soda?" the other commentator suggested. He shuffled through his papers like he was looking for the answer in his script, then shrugged.

"Soda water," Rosette said, her sobs leveling off. "It's soda water gets blood out. You boys need to give me and Alfie a moment," she said. "We have some praying to do." She reached up and traced her finger around the hole where the turkey's neck would have been, then dipped a finger in up to the knuckle, then another.

The room felt swollen. In the slatted light falling through the curtains and onto the couch I thought I saw something wriggle beneath the turkey's skin. Rosette held up her hand and the wet grease dripped slowly from the tip of her finger down toward her palm. She rubbed her thumb and forefinger together.

We took our skateboards and headed for the Ditch, still in our church clothes. Charleston walked in front of me without looking back. When we got to the Ditch he dropped in and I watched him carve fast and high for a moment before I followed. He kept his wheels on the concrete, letting his fingertips trace the weeds at the tops of the walls.

Halfway down the length of the Ditch I popped an ollie at the top of a wall and floated, watching my shadow below me, my knees pulled up, the board stuck to my feet by some miracle of physics. I still don't understand how we went around defying gravity like that, then expecting it to hold us to the ground. I wished Charleston could have seen it. I never landed that trick again.

I carved behind Charleston to the end of the Ditch and slid on the tail of my skateboard, wearing down the already thin wood against the concrete. He was bent over with his hands on his knees. "Creek's rising," he said, and I tried to figure where the water was coming from. Maybe the construction had freed up a spring somewhere, redirected water that had been flowing to another source. It wasn't yet up to the sandy banks, to the concrete pillars under the bridge graffitied with declarations of love and regret, but it was close.

ROSETTE DIDN'T TRY HARD TO COVER HERSELF WHEN WE walked in. She pulled a thin white sheet over her chest. Rancid turkey grease had turned the sheet translucent, and I could see her brown nipples through the fabric. Her hair had fallen out of a loose ponytail and down around her shoulders. "Oh, Lord," Rosette said, smiling. "Don't you boys know how to knock?" She lit a cigarette.

The bird slumped on the couch, flies crawling in and out of the hole where its neck used to be. Several cans of Alfie's beer were crumpled on the brown carpet. Charleston stomped up the stairs to his room and collapsed onto his bed with a loud thump that shook the ceiling. The bird stretched a little and settled against Rosette's chest. Rosette rested an arm along the back of the couch, the cigarette smoking between her fingers. Flies crawled up her arm and she didn't try to swat them away. The couch, slick with grease, caught light from the TV and took on the general hues of what was happening onscreen: green, gray, blue.

Rosette saw me watching her cigarette and held her pack out to me. "Want one?" she asked. I'd never smoked before but I'd seen it done enough to know how to put it between my lips, how to lean over her when she flicked the lighter, how to inhale the flame into the tip, how to wait until the end of the cigarette turned to ember before pulling away.

Leaning in, I smelled rot under the stale smoke and beer. I coughed hard with my first drag and Rosette placed her thumb in the spot between my eyes and stroked it down the bridge of my nose. "It gets easier," she said. "Just breathe."

I couldn't take my eyes off the bird, the flies crawling in and out of its neck hole, the bones inside the cavity illuminated by the ambient light in the room, the meat flecked with thick red blood clots, the skin sagging where the meat underneath had started to liquify. The turkey turned and stretched its tiny, withered wing toward me, lovingly I think. I jerked away, banged into the coffee table, spilling a beer can onto its side. "It's okay, baby," Rosette said. "Mama will wipe it up."

I smoked that cigarette down to the filter standing

between the couch and the TV, watching the ember burn closer to my fingers. When it was as far down as it would go Rosette held out an empty beer can with black ash around the rim and I dropped the smoldering nub down into it. The butt sizzled in the last bit of beer at the bottom.

"You go on to bed," Rosette said. "It's been a big day for all of us. Alfie's tired from crossing over." The bird crossed its arms over its chest and seemed to nod as much as it could nod without a neck or a head. Rosette traced her fingers over its breast muscles, down the line at the center of its chest where the skin had knitted together.

I took the stairs quietly, not wanting to wake up Charleston, but he was awake, with his shirt off, his chest white and untanned. A tuft of black hair poked out of the waistband of his gym shorts. His church clothes were in a pile next to the bed. "You were smoking," he said.

I nodded.

"Why would you do that?"

I didn't know why. My grandmother had died of lung cancer. I already felt an itch in my brain that hadn't been there before. Charleston shook his head and turned away, picking up a book from the floor, a history of a country too far away to dream of visiting.

I took off my polo shirt and khaki pants and stood in my underwear. Charleston's back was covered with moles that could have been the beginnings of skin cancer. I got into bed and pulled the covers up to my chin, turning toward him. I looked closely at moles left behind from childhood sunburns and tried to see whether they were irregularly shaped, whether they might be growing, whether their edges were expanding in pink patches, growing outward to contaminate the rest of his skin, growing inward toward his blood and bones. The light from the reading lamp was dim and strained my eyes. I fell asleep this way and dreamed of a landscape continuously reformed, a place where the ground never settled.

KINGDOM OF
THE WOUNDED

Melody and Erica found the purple castle the night before, hidden in some cedar trees, while they were on acid. Melody's ex-boyfriend Amos was in there, they said. Amos had been dead over a year. His blood still stained the beige carpet in Dario's house, where we bought our drugs. We told each other it had been a mistake, that Amos didn't know the gun was loaded, but Dario's guns were always loaded.

I drove and Erica told me where to turn, leaning into the front seat, putting her head between me and Melody. "Right at the manatee mailbox," she said, pointing at a mailbox in the shape of a manatee, its flippers held out, ready for deliveries. There was an open gate across the dirt road with tall grass growing through its frame where it hung crooked, angled toward the ground. It had not been shut in a long time. "Park by the fence," Erica said. Her jaw clenched and unclenched in a chemical jitter. She smiled, her lips barely stretching across her teeth.

I was in love with Melody, with the way she handled tragedy, the way she wore clothes that were too small for her, the way she perfumed the car with skincare products and cheap cigarettes. Erica made me uncomfortable, but she and Melody circled each other like debris being sucked down a drain.

There was a trailer off to the side of the road that looked uninhabited, its front steps rotted through and collapsing. A light over the door blinked off and on like an alarm or a beacon. Melody held onto my arm as we walked through weeds so high they brushed against our thighs. A barbed wire fence ran beside the road and we climbed through as Erica held the wires apart. Melody wore a black skirt, and as she bent to weave herself through the fence I saw bruises on her smooth and shiny legs. My pants caught a barb that pricked my skin as I followed her through. On this side of the fence, a cluster of cedars rose thin and straight beyond a cow pasture. When we reached the tree line I could see red bark peeling off the trunks like scabs.

Melody grabbed Erica's hand. "It's still there," she said.

It took me a moment to recognize what I was looking at because the shape was so out of place. A small castle stood in the middle of the trees. It was only six or seven feet tall, with towers in the corners and battlements stubbing its walls. Its bright purple paint was chipping to show concrete gray underneath. Melody and Erica waited on either side of the arched doorway, beckoning me inside.

I dipped my head to pass through the door. The ceiling was low enough that I had to stay bent at the waist. The inside smelled moist, like something dragged out of a lake. Amos sat at the other end of the small space in an aluminum folding chair with his hands in his lap. "Did you bring cigarettes?" he asked. My hand went to my pocket and I took out a crushed pack with only one cigarette left, flipped upside down for good luck. I held it in my open palm.

Amos took the cigarette and stuck it between his lips. I sparked my lighter and the small flame illuminated the missing left side of his head, where the bullet had exited his skull. Flies crawled on the crusted skin at the edges of the wound. He looked the same, except his features were slightly out of place, shifted to the side. His eyes caught mine as he inhaled and the tip of the cigarette burned.

Erica laughed and I turned to see Melody handing her a metal bowl. Erica took a hit. "Fucking crazy, right?" she said, holding the smoke in her lungs as she spoke.

"Ask him something," Melody said. Smoke leaked out from between her lips.

"Ask him?"

She nodded and licked her pink lip gloss. She stepped toward me, standing very close, her head almost on my shoulder. Her brown eyes looked black in the dark.

"Something you really want to know," Erica said. She took another hit off the metal bowl and coughed, wheezing out the last of her breath. Melody put her hand in the middle of my back and pushed me closer to Amos. Cigarette smoke rose from the hole in the side of his head.

"What's it like on the other side?" I asked, looking down at my shoes.

"You can tell it's all fake," he said. He lifted his hand and gestured at the concrete wall.

Melody exhaled on the side of my neck, her breath floral and mildewed. "Ask him about the future," she whispered in my ear.

Amos stomped his cigarette and reached out for another. I showed him my empty pack. "Can you see the future?" I asked.

"Sure," he said, reaching up to scratch the edge of the exit wound. "I can see all kinds of things I never wanted to see."

I had exams the next day at school. I hadn't studied or attended classes for most of the semester. "What's on the exam tomorrow?" I asked. "Can you give me the answers, or does it have to be some kind of cryptic thing?"

Amos laughed. His mouth hung open too far. Nothing held his jaw in place. "Don't worry about the test, man," he said.

I wasn't worried about the test, but my parents had impressed on me the value of an education. I didn't see a future in academics. The lessons I had learned from books felt like they were written for other people. "Like, don't worry about it because I'll do well, or don't worry about it for some other reason?"

Amos gave me the kind of pitying smile that means you're about to figure something out for yourself. "Does Dario still have the best drugs?" he asked.

I looked back at Melody. Her lips shined with flavored gloss. She nodded. "Yeah, he's still got the best drugs," I said.

"I miss good drugs," Amos said. "Everything here is like a cardboard cutout of what you expect it to be. Everything here gives you little paper cuts."

Melody put her hand on my shoulder. Erica took another hit from the bowl. I wanted to ask Amos more questions, like why he did what he did with the gun, but I was embarrassed. I guess Amos could see I was starting to get restless, because he politely slapped his thighs. "Okay," he said, "thanks for coming." He didn't stand up from the folding chair as we left the castle. The sun had gone down. Melody and Erica held my hands to guide me through the cedar trees and to the cow pasture, where the moon lit the way to the car.

Dario's house was in the suburbs. His backyard was brown dirt because no grass would grow in the shade of two wide oak trees. His parents had left him the house and when they died in prison he took over their drug distribution network. We weren't big customers, but we'd known each other since middle school so he let us keep coming around, even after Amos died, when other people stopped partying at the house because of the bloodstains and because the police started driving by all the time, parking down the street, making note of the cars that came and went.

That night I sat between the girls on the white leather couch in the white-tiled living room while Dario paced and peeked out the blinds every few minutes. Gas masks were lined up on the windowsill facing the street and rifles leaned in the corners. He was always saying if the cops ever came to the door that he was going to die shooting, and I knew that he would. We didn't tell him about Amos. The girls and I hadn't spoken about it directly, but we knew Dario wouldn't handle the Amos thing well. They had been best friends.

Amos's bloodstain was in a small den off the living room. As we waited for Dario to divvy out the pills and tabs I stared into the dark spot through the open door. It looked like a chasm had opened in the carpet. I picked at the peeling leather couch.

"This is good stuff," Dario said, opening a jewelry bag of white powder and inhaling a little bit from his overgrown pinky nail. "It's clean, though, so be careful. A dab will do you."

My head felt too clear. I could see everything that was happening in the room at once: Melody pulling on her eyelashes, Erica licking her teeth, Dario looking back and forth between us.

"Did you guys take those yellow tabs the other night?"

"Yeah," Erica said. "It was pretty medieval." Melody put her hand on Erica's forearm to quiet her. The gesture looked loving in the slivered moonlight coming through the blinds.

Dario smiled. "That's great," he said, rubbing a sad strip of hair on his jawline. "They had me feeling out of place, too." He gestured at a line of red gas cans against the sliding door to the back yard. They were brand new, with price tags still on them, but I didn't need to ask to know they were all full.

Melody clapped and bounced on the couch. "Is that a project?" she asked.

Dario nodded. He always had a project going, because he didn't sleep and didn't leave the house much. "I can't tell you about that," he said, looking at the front window, then walking quickly toward it and pulling the blinds slightly apart to peek out onto the street. "The HOA has been on my ass lately. Are you wearing a wire?" He fingered something in his waistband that I'm sure was a handgun.

Melody smiled and lifted her shirt. A too-small black bra cut into the tops of her breasts. I wanted to stare but looked away at the oak trees in the back yard, past the red gas cans.

"That's good," Dario said. "You ask too many questions, you know?" He patted her on the head and her hair-sprayed curls bounced right back.

"I love projects," Melody said.

Dario handed her the sandwich bag of drugs. "Come see me when you're out."

We stepped out the front door and into a yard overgrown with weeds. It always felt warm and good to leave Dario's house because he kept the air conditioning cold, to keep the humidity down so moisture didn't spoil the drugs hidden in closets and cupboards and safes.

We got a hotel room by the freeway at a rundown chain that let teenagers pay in cash. Melody and Erica took turns putting tabs and pills on my tongue, then meeting guys in the parking lot to sell off some of the drugs we'd bought, leaning into driver's side windows, coming back with handfuls of money and stacking it on the faux-wood table.

I kept taking more tabs and pills whenever the girls told me to open my mouth, but I didn't feel anything. Sometimes the drugs Dario gave us were fake. Melody and Erica went to the bathroom together every half hour or so. Their pupils got wider as the night went on. We lay on the bed, the comforter scratchy against our bare skin, and watched TV with the sound off. Melody held my hand on one side and Erica held my hand on the other. They vibrated just a little when they inhaled, drawing breath for too long, like they might overinflate. They rested their heads on my shoulders. When cars pulled into the parking lot Melody stood up with a smile, looked out through the curtains to see if they were customers. Her phone buzzed on the bedside table.

Each time she answered it, Erica traced a finger on the inside of my elbow and looked up at me, but I kept my eyes on the TV, where a talk show host reached over to grab the exposed thigh of his guest, part of a gag I couldn't understand without sound. She slapped his hand but his fingers crept back across the desk toward her, over and over, and she became visibly uncomfortable until the show cut to commercial.

The next morning I woke up early. The girls were still asleep as I slipped out of the room and closed the heavy door behind me. I tried to look in through the window, putting my forehead against the glass, closing one eye and staring at the crack between the curtains, but I couldn't see anything. The room was dark. I knew the girls would sleep past checkout.

I was still in school, but Melody and Erica had informally dropped out by then. They stopped going and the school stopped calling. I pulled my car onto a country road, the sky in my rearview brightening but the sky in front of me still dark blue. The road to the purple castle went by and I thought about turning around but kept going straight, toward the school and the exams I knew I would fail.

A silver sedan passed me too fast, swerving in and out of traffic. The air sucked out of my open window as the car rushed by and it felt like a shockwave in my chest. A few car lengths ahead the sedan became a flash, catching the morning sunlight as it spun sideways and rolled, showing its undercarriage, then its shattered windshield, before disappearing into a cloud of dust and steam.

The car was destroyed. It was upside down, its engine

exposed like a ribcage. Books and papers fluttered and stuck to the dewy grass. I got out of my car and turned one of the books over with my toe, not knowing what to do.

"Oh God," a girl moaned from the tree line past the ditch. "My head."

I found her with her head nestled in the crook of a tree, where the trunk branched into two. I had civics class with her but didn't know her name. "Are you okay?" I said.

"I can't move," she said. "I want to move, but I can't move." I watched her arms and legs not moving.

I didn't see any signs of trauma. She wasn't bleeding. Her clothes were dirty but she was dressed in pastels that felt seasonally appropriate. She looked up at me. "Oh God," she said. "I'm swelling. There's not enough space inside me."

I know that my memory here is false, impossible, but I remember her head growing like a water balloon, pushing her hairline away from her eyes, spreading her eyebrows apart. I was afraid she would pop.

Although I didn't register it right away, our beloved civics teacher had stopped her car in the middle of the road. She pushed through the gathering crowd and knelt at the girl's side.

"Look at my eyes," our beloved civics teacher said. "The ambulance is coming. You aren't going to pop. There will be plenty of room inside you to swell and then shrink again. Try to picture your own elasticity. Think of all the things you learned for your exams today. Remember how we studied the branches of government, how one might get bloated, taking up space constitutionally intended for another branch, but how there is a system in place to put things back into their correct proportions? Remember how we discussed that things naturally seek balance? What would you say is the primary mechanism that maintains balance?" The girl's eyes fluttered. "Think, now," our beloved civics teacher said. "This will be on the exam."

The girl with her head in the crook of the tree opened her eyes and said, "Congressional budget approval."

Our beloved civics teacher reached out and touched the girl's cheek, careful not to move her neck. "That's one correct answer," she said. "Budget oversight is a powerful tool."

A line of cars stopped on the road. People leaned out their windows, their eyes squinting against the rising sun, trying to see what had happened. No one seemed to notice me backing away, getting in my car, turning around, heading in the opposite direction of the school. There was nothing I was going to be able to write on my exams that would make me forget the way the girl's head looked in the crook of that tree.

I turned off the country road and pulled down the driveway to the purple castle and parked. Parting the barbed wire by myself was difficult but I made it through with only a few scratches on my arms and back.

Amos was in the same place on the aluminum folding chair. "Gave up on exams?" He held out his hands for a cigarette. I shook one out of my pack and lit it for him. "That girl is going to be fine," he said. "You would have failed your exams anyway." I nodded and sat down on the dirt floor of the castle with my back to the wall. "You're in love with Melody," he said, looking past me, out the arched doorway. "I knew the gun was loaded."

"Do you feel different now?" I asked. "Better?"

Amos shrugged. His posture was too loose. I remembered the way he would get excited when listening to music, bringing his fist in front of his face to sing along with his favorite parts. "It's not like it's some big relief," he said. "There are just other problems now."

That was what I expected him to say. I could see into the hole in his skull where his brain used to be. Skin and bone jutted from the sides of the opening in jagged points. A green lizard cautiously climbed up his shoulder and perched on the shattered edge with its tail hanging down into his head. The lizard extended a red flap of skin on its neck, retracted it, then extended it again, the same way I had seen thousands of other lizards do thousands of times before.

THE CULLING

was blackout drunk the night of the attack. Behind our house an open field led to the library. I liked to sit on the back porch drinking beer, looking at the orange glow of the lights in the library's parking lot. A young woman had been returning a book after hours when the kid with the blank stare grabbed her and dragged her out to the field, among the oak trees and chunks of concrete and illegally dumped sofas. I don't think I saw or heard anything, but there were a lot of nights I don't remember back then. I have to admit to myself that I could have heard the young woman struggling, the pounding of flesh on flesh, the quiet breaking of teeth, and done nothing.

When I woke up in the morning, hungover and sweaty, the field was full of police standing around taking notes. I took my coffee out on the back porch and waved. A skinny cop walked over and stopped at the edge of our yard. "Did you see anything out here last night?"

I squinted. "No, nothing. What's going on?" The coffee turned in my stomach. I tried not to retch.

"I don't think you want your kids to see." He pointed to the window, where the twins cupped their eyes against the glass. In the middle of the field, paramedics lifted the young woman's broken body onto a stretcher.

She had been a volunteer at an animal shelter. It seemed like she was going to die, but she held on, comatose, her family sitting vigil. They brought pictures of her favorite animals from the shelter and lined them up beside her. Footage from the nightly news showed basset hounds and cats and pet rabbits watching over her. A reporter reminded us that these kinds of attacks were unusual where we lived, that we should feel sad for the young woman and her family, but we should use that sadness as motivation to reinvest in our community.

I came to recognize the kid with the blank stare from the videos of his arrest and interrogation. His mouth always hung open. His eyes always looked unfocused. He had been beaten by his stepdad as a child. The news speculated brain damage might have caused him to have elevated levels of aggression.

The week after the attack a group of us—dads with beer bellies spilling over our cargo shorts—formed a neighborhood watch. We congregated at the end of the cul-de-sac to discuss our findings with men whose names I barely knew. A shady character from the trailer park down the street had been seen riding through the neighborhood on a bicycle with a bent frame. Iguanas had begun encroaching into the neighborhood from the tall grass in the field behind our houses. The unusually wet summer had given mosquitoes ample puddles for breeding. We'd been slow to bring our garbage cans in from the street, and we promised to do better. We wanted to keep our street clean.

At the end of the summer a hurricane blew past. It was not a direct hit, but close enough that it knocked down power lines and old oak trees already in the process of dying. The debris put holes in some of the neighbors' roofs. While the power was out, we took shifts walking up and down the street with flashlights, looking for outsiders we thought might have the capacity for violence. There were more cats and iguanas than ever. I oiled my silver revolver and thought about buying floodlights, but my back yard and the open field beyond stayed dark.

IT WAS STILL HOT A MONTH LATER, ON HALLOWEEN, AND our twins sweated through their face paint, black cat whiskers and green iguana scales melting onto the collars of their shirts. One of the twins had long fake cat's claws, while the other had a felt tail pinned to the back of her pants that twisted as though it was partially severed. I don't know why they picked nuisance animals for costumes. They waited by the door, holding their empty bags, while my wife and I put our shoes on.

Our son was too old to dress up. He had just started driving.

"You have to watch for little kids tonight," I told him, putting my hand on his shoulder. "They blend into the environment."

My son nodded, his lips pressed together to show he was taking the new responsibility seriously. When he was little I used to crush his hands in mine, as a joke, grating his bones back and forth on each other, just to make him squirm. I looked back with regret on all the times he had reached up to hold my hand in traffic, or to feel safe on theme park rides, and I had squeezed him until it hurt.

I didn't crush the twins' hands like that. I was learning from some of my mistakes.

My wife and I walked behind the twins, drinking cans of warm beer. The block was still lined with trees downed in the hurricane. We had to step into the street where fallen oaks blocked the sidewalk. I finished one of the beers and crushed the can under my foot, then slipped it into my pocket. The metal poked my thigh and the last few drops leaked onto my leg.

We approached a house with an astroturf lawn. Their Christmas decorations were still up from the previous year, but they were accessorized for Halloween. Santa Claus wore a witch hat. Rudolph had fake blood dripping from his mouth. When a woman in a genie costume opened the door, the twins stood silently, holding their bags open. They were shy.

"Trick or treat," I reminded them to say.

"Trick or treat," the twins said, hesitantly. Their face paint had deformed, making it hard to tell what they were supposed to be.

"Are you a witch?" the woman in the genie costume asked my daughter who was dressed as a cat. My daughter nodded, uncomfortable correcting the woman. "You're a very good witch. And are you a frog?"

My other daughter shook her head. "An iguana," she said, turning so the woman could see her tail.

"Oh yes, I see it now," the woman said. "Very good." She started dumping handfuls of candy into the girls' bags. "It's getting late. Take the rest of it." They looked up at her in wonder. The woman in the genie costume tilted her head toward the empty field and the library, where the lights in the parking lot had already come on for the night. "We don't want you cuties out after dark."

SOME THINGS I LEARNED FROM NEWS COVERAGE OF THE kid with the blank stare in the aftermath of the attack:

His stepfather was an unemployed minor-league short stop forced into retirement by a series of knee and elbow injuries. His mom had two jobs, so the kid and stepdad spent a lot of time together. The stepdad had a strong arm, the news said, from his years on the baseball field. Social services had visited the home but never found any bruises large enough to warrant further action.

The kid with the blank stare had attended the same high school as my son. His teachers remembered him as quiet. He sat in the back corner of his classes, arms crossed, refusing to do any work. He got expelled a year before the attack for an incident involving a cow heart.

The cow heart incident played out as follows: He got his hands on a cow heart and smuggled it to school. He smashed it against a bathroom wall and let it slide down to the tiled floor. The school was put on lockdown. Administration feared it was the beginning of a school shooting. The students stayed hidden, huddled in corners and closets, until the police cleared the building.

He got caught because his backpack was soaked through with blood. DNA tests confirmed it was animal blood.

The kid's mom never left his stepdad. The press got pictures of them walking into the courtroom together, his hand at the base of her neck.

His favorite color was yellow. When he was twelve he begged his mom to repaint his room yellow, to buy him all yellow clothes for school, but she could only afford one yellow outfit. He wore the outfit at least twice a week, running the wash himself to make sure it was clean.

Kids at school picked on him because of the sound of his laugh. He was an eager student when he was young but in middle school he started having stomach aches every week that kept him home. His teachers wouldn't let him make up the work he had missed.

A few months before the library attack, the kid was arrested for sneaking in the back door of a fast food restaurant after closing. The employees had left the door open as they carried bags of trash from the kitchen out to the dumpster. The kid locked himself in the office with the closing manager, pulled a long filet knife out of a sheath tucked into his waistband, and held it to her throat while he put his hands on her body.

The state decided not to press charges against the kid with the blank stare because he agreed to rehabilitation and therapy. His therapists remembered him as a quietly angry patient. Nothing that couldn't be treated with medication, they had written in their reports.

The kid with the blank stare loved his grandmother so much that at her funeral he refused to let the casket be lowered into the grave. The kid's mom waited with him while he stood at the edge of the grave and growled at the undertakers. Eventually she had to drag him away, but the kid pulled so hard against her that she was afraid she would dislocate his shoulder. He screamed the whole way home.

THE WOMAN IN THE GENIE COSTUME HAD UNSETTLED US.
We steered the twins back toward home, plastic grocery
bags bulging at their sides. Back at the house they counted
out their candy on the living room floor. "How many can
we have?" my iguana daughter asked.

"As many as you want," my wife said. Halloween was
her favorite holiday. Even though she was worried about
refined sugar, she couldn't bring herself to regulate their
candy intake.

"Which kind is your favorite, Daddy?" my cat daughter
asked. I pointed to the chocolate-covered caramels. She
grabbed all that she could see and put them in my hand like
an offering. There was so much goodness in my children,
more than I could ever have taught them. Being near them
made me feel scooped out, like the inside of a pumpkin
ready for carving.

I sent them to get their showers, with specific
instructions to scrub the face paint off so they wouldn't go
to school the next day still looking a little bit like a cat and
an iguana, which might make their teachers think less of
me as a parent. They left their candy spread on the floor,
categorized into piles. My wife checked the location of our
son's phone. He was still at his girlfriend's house. I left her
alone on the couch and went to the back porch to keep
drinking.

The lights from the library parking lot shimmered
across the field. I drank a beer quickly and then grabbed
two more from a cooler full of melted ice water. I imagined
what it would have looked like to see the kid with the blank
stare attacking that poor young woman. Their silhouettes

would have looked like the piles of concrete and small oak trees scattered throughout the field. I imagined grabbing my silver revolver from its place by the bed, slipping my shoes on so the sandspurs didn't stab my feet, and charging out into the field full of righteous justice.

My daughter who had been dressed as a cat knocked on the sliding glass door and pressed her face to it. Her hair was wet from the shower. A little bit of black face paint was visible at her hair line. "Good night, Daddy," she said through the door. I smiled and waved my beer can at her.

My drinking had gotten worse since the attack. It had been so close to our house, to our kids. I felt like a failure. I made my fingers into the shape of a pistol and pointed them at a silhouette in the field, then I let my head rest against the back of the chair and closed my eyes.

THE CATS KEPT COMING TO OUR NEIGHBORHOOD BECAUSE one of our elderly neighbors fed them, dumping can after can of wet food in her back yard every night. The cats got pregnant and had kittens. The bird and squirrel populations dropped to almost nothing. I tried to warn her that sooner or later some of our neighbors would call animal control. The shelter didn't have space to hold them all. The cats would have to be put down, I told her.

She shrugged. "I can't look at hungry cats and do nothing," she said.

When the animal control trucks pulled into the neighborhood, she shut her blinds and didn't go out to check her mailbox until after they left.

The iguanas were new to the area, pets that had been

released into the wild. We weren't prepared for the strange sight of them, climbing the trunks of palm trees. The cats didn't know what to make of them either. If a cat tried sneaking up on one, the iguana would lash out with its long tail. The neighborhood filled with the sounds of hissing iguanas. It became common to see them postured aggressively with their chests displayed. After a while the cats seemed to give up. They watched the iguanas warily, without trying to pounce.

The iguanas burrowed around the edges of the neighbors' decorative backyard goldfish ponds, causing structural damage that prevented them from holding water. Their landscaping bills, already high from keeping the natural weeds at bay, grew even higher. Some of the neighbors started to wonder if it was worth even having decorative goldfish ponds at all. They had seemed like such a good idea once, a place to sit and read, but they rarely sat and read. The gurgling sounds of the water pumps were nice, but the water pumps frequently burned out, and the decorative goldfish ponds became breeding grounds for mosquitos, and the goldfish died, and their back yards stank of dead fish.

WHEN I OPENED MY EYES THE LIVING ROOM LIGHT WAS out and my nose was filled with the iron smell of blood. Shapes in the field were moving. I was stumbling drunk but knew I had to do something. I stood up, swaying back and forth, listening closely. Traffic from the road, the sound of a neighbor's TV. Underneath it all, I thought I heard a muffled cry for help.

It was happening again. My daughters were just a few feet away.

I threw the sliding glass door open and ran inside. My shoulder slammed hard into the doorframe as I entered the bedroom. I pulled the silver revolver down from the closet shelf, tested its weight in each hand. I spun the cylinder. Every chamber was loaded. I had never held it with such purpose.

I hadn't noticed my wife in bed, reading the twins a story they loved about ghosts that were nice even though they were dead. "Do I need to call the police?" she asked.

"Do not call the police," I said. "Daddy has work to do."

My wife closed the book and pulled the twins closer to her. I turned around before she had time to respond and bumped into the door frame again on the way out of the room. It was hard to make my way through the living room, dodging the coffee table and ottoman and the corners of the couch, but I managed to stay upright, using my free hand to catch myself when I started to fall. I ran out the back and stood at the edge of the yard. The border between our property and the open field was marked by where I stopped mowing the grass.

I stood still, listening, the revolver pointed toward the sky. The smell of blood was strong and I licked my teeth to make sure it wasn't just my swollen gums. My eyes scanned the field, looking for signs of movement. As headlights passed on the road the shadows of stunted oak trees and overgrown weeds shifted. I started moving forward, swinging the gun from side to side, tripping in holes dug by animals, holes where the stumps of trees once were, holes where construction crews had gathered fill dirt to level the yards of our neighborhood. I tried to step quietly but my feet were heavy. I had been taught to practice good trigger discipline, to keep my finger pressed against the barrel, to keep the barrel pointed at the ground, but I aimed the revolver at every rustle of tall grass. My finger curled inward. In the brief quiet between passing cars I heard slapping, growling. I pointed the gun at the sound.

Righteousness swelled in my chest. If you had asked me, even in that very moment, I would have told you I hated violence, but the truth is I was electrified by the possibility of hurting someone, of saving someone. This was my neighborhood, I told myself. Where my children played. Where I trusted the flimsy locks on our doors and windows to keep us safe. Sometimes it is a father's responsibility to break something to preserve something else. Love is an act of destruction, I told myself, but I didn't really believe it. I just wanted to hear the gunshot, to feel the recoil.

Something hissed and grunted at my side. My eyes hadn't fully adjusted to the dark, and I could only see dark shapes twisting among the tall grass. I tried to picture the kid with the blank stare, the shape of his shoulders, the shape of his skull.

I heard movement to my left, turned, and pulled the trigger. The muzzle flashed and the shot rang in my ears. A black cat scrambled to its feet and took off running. An iguana lay twitching in the sand with its head mostly severed.

ONCE AN INVASIVE SPECIES TAKES HOLD IT IS NEARLY impossible to eradicate it. I dreamed of fish that jump six feet out of the water, concussing the drivers of passing boats. I dreamed of flies that spread incurable disease to citrus farms. I dreamed of snakes six feet long that choke out alligators in the swamp. I could never kill them all.

There are countries to the south where iguanas are part of the ecosystem, are not invasive, have more natural predators. I'd wanted to learn how to live with the creatures, but our county employed men to hunt the iguanas down. They piled corpses in the backs of pickup trucks and burned them in large bonfires.

In those countries to the south iguanas are known as the chicken of the tree. Their meat, though filled with tiny prickling bones, tastes pleasant and mild. Sometimes they are cooked in a coconut milk curry. Sometimes they are fried.

My grandmother pan-fried frog legs when I was a kid. She taught me to fire a shotgun in the air near an eagle's nest, to scare it off so the government didn't show up and catalog the nest, making the land around it protected and unusable. I remember her in the rocking chair on her porch, scanning the sky for eagles, the double-barrel shotgun leaning in the corner behind her.

I CARRIED THE IGUANA INTO THE HOUSE. ITS HEAD WAS barely attached. I had somehow, despite my drunkenness and the near-total darkness, managed to deliver a killing shot directly to its neck. Its eyes were open. I cradled it gently so it wouldn't break apart.

My wife and the twins were in the living room, standing by the door.

"We heard something loud," my daughter who had been dressed as an iguana said.

"I called the cops," my wife said.

I wasn't mad, even though I had just illegally discharged a firearm. I set the revolver down on the counter and hugged her with my free hand. She let me hug her, but she was stiff and didn't hug me back. The room smelled like gunpowder. The barrel of the revolver pointed at the front door of the house. Later, when I picked up the gun to store it, I noticed it was cocked and another round was ready to fire.

I slapped the iguana carcass on the cutting board and grabbed a can of beer from the fridge. My eyes lazily doubled and drifted out of focus. I knew I couldn't finish the beer, but I gulped it nonetheless.

"This is a Halloween miracle," I told my wife and the twins, who had assembled in front of me. "I have to make sure this iguana's death serves a purpose. I'm going to make a stew."

"I am both morally and practically opposed to the making of a stew," my wife said. "It's past the kids' bedtime and they ate so much candy they nearly vomited. They are already going to have nightmares from all this." She waved her hand at the gun and the iguana. "I don't want them to watch."

I had the sick urge to put my hand inside the iguana's neck and animate the head, making its mouth open and close as I spoke in a silly voice. "What's wrong?" I might have it say. "Don't you think I'm handsome?"

The counter was smeared with blood and innards. The scene wasn't appropriate for children. I shrugged and hugged the twins with the inside of my forearm to avoid getting iguana blood on their pajamas.

I'd never seen an animal butchered before, but I grabbed a long kitchen knife and started cutting open the iguana, sorting the things I found inside into parts I thought looked edible and parts I thought looked inedible. My grandmother had tried to teach me to butcher the quails she shot in the strawberry fields outside her house, but I hadn't paid close attention.

My wife sat on the couch, looking at me over the top of her phone screen. The revolver lay between us on the kitchen counter.

I didn't know what I was doing. It was ridiculous, that I thought I could make a stew. The iguana's death had been a waste, and I felt ashamed. My grandmother had taught me never to waste an animal's death, but I was too drunk to cook anything. The iguana lay splayed on the cutting board, its four legs stretched outward, its belly torn open, the underside of its chin suggesting a head raised in prayer.

My son came home, right on time, just before his curfew. He was a conscientious kid, observant of our rules and the rules of his teachers. He didn't notice the revolver on the counter, pointing at him as he took off his shoes. "How was your Halloween?" I asked him, speaking too loudly to cover up my own embarrassment.

"I drove slow," he said. "My girlfriend could tell how much I care about the safety of children."

I saw a hickey by the collar of his shirt, but I didn't say anything. I was changing. I wanted him to have the experience of being a teenager, the high-water marks fueled by hormones and overactive sweat glands, the unbearable tension, the constant transgression. I leaned on him and fell off balance.

"It's important to respect the speed limit," I said.

He stepped back and looked at the counter. "You taught me that," he said. "I always maintain a safe following distance behind the car in front of me."

The remains of the iguana were a horrible mess, with strands of guts and splatters of blood drying to crisp flakes on the countertop. In the morning I would take down a bottle of bleach and address the problem. In the morning I would be a little bit better. I would put the gun in the closet. I wouldn't drag things in from the yard and butcher them on the counter. I would want to be the kind of person who could change. I crawled into bed with iguana blood caked on my skin. I couldn't be the kind of person I wanted to be. I lay in the dark, the room spinning. I couldn't be anyone except who I was.

SEPTIC

Y ou're just waiting to die," my wife said, nudging me with her toe. "Try to make it less obvious. For the kids' sake."

I lifted my face from the pool deck and closed one eye in order to focus. In the large window facing our back patio I could see my children, shirtless, eating their cereal, dribbling milk onto their pink bellies. My mouth was coated in the chalky paste of undissolved pills. I licked my teeth, checking to see if they were where I expected them to be. The pool water was a deep, opaque green. Trailing away from me, a line of thick red vomit had started to congeal. An empty plastic vodka bottle bobbed on the surface of the pool. The supportive white underwear they'd given me to wear after my vasectomy was stained green with algae. I must have been swimming. My wife shook her head and went inside.

A few minutes later she and the kids pulled out of the driveway in our minivan. A long gash ran down the side panel where I had clipped a guard rail. I waved, but I couldn't tell through the tinted windows if they waved back. As the van rounded the corner I stuck my hand into my underwear to peel the damp fabric away from my genitals. My neighbors passed by, walking their dogs, politely pretending they didn't see me.

I put on some clothes and sat down at my desk. I hadn't written a word in years, though I kept telling myself I was a writer. My last book had nearly bankrupted my publisher. Several boxes of unsold copies were stacked in the corner of my office, leaning as though they might collapse.

"We can't afford to pay you," my publisher had written, "but you can at least take some of these copies off our hands. Why we ever agreed to take on this project is a mystery to those of us still left after the round of layoffs in the wake of this disaster. May we remind you that you refused to do even simple things, such as answering emails and phone calls. We will write these copies of the book off as a loss and pretend they were burned in a dumpster fire.

"Consider this a termination of your contract, a relinquishment from any responsibilities not yet met, absolution for the sin of poor judgment on both our parts. We hope your future endeavors and ours will not be colored by the stink of this literary failure, which we call literary only by the broadest possible definition of that term, because it does not rise to any reasonable person's standard of literature.

"We don't think you're a bad person. You have been, at times, charming. You have written a good sentence here and there. We recommend, if you are just waiting to die, that you refrain from publishing detailed accounts of that process. It's depressing. Remember that we once cared about you."

I had been leaving the unsold books everywhere I went, putting them in places where I knew the rain would ruin them. While running errands I'd leave copies against gas pumps, near trash cans, where they could be easily thrown away. I'd take the family to the beach and bring a handful of copies to leave at the water line, where the waves would carry them away. This was littering, I knew, and the fact that I was cluttering up beautiful places contributed to my shame.

So there was a lot on my mind as I tried to start writing.

"My fat fingers stumbled across the keyboard," I wrote, which was as good of an opening line as I could come up with. I looked at that for a moment, then deleted it. The first try always falls short.

"My fat fingers poked at the keyboard," I wrote, then deleted it immediately.

"My fat fingers crushed the keys. No one expects the fatness of one's fingers to affect the way they type, but it does."

A lot had gone into writing those couple of sentences. I stood up from the writing desk and went to the back patio to drink beer and stare at the weeds I hadn't mowed. I needed to be surrounded by things I should have already done. It was almost noon. I opened another can of beer and tried to think about the sentence, about the fat fingers, interrogating the image, to see where it would lead me. By the time the kids got home from school I was drunk and no closer to discovering why fat fingers might be an important character detail. I stumbled into the living room to greet them.

"Daddy, why are you falling into the bookshelf?" my daughter asked. Kids always get right to the heart of the thing.

"I had a hard day writing," I said. She gave me a hug. Her dependence on me threatened to pull me through the floor and into the center of the earth.

My wife shook her head. She looked so beautiful and disappointed standing in the kitchen. If I could have changed, I would have. I didn't want to be the kind of person who failed everyone and everything. When I was young, I dreamed I would one day be successful at something. It was a stupid thing to dream.

"What do you guys want for dinner?" my wife asked the kids.

"Macaroni and cheese," the kids said, all together, as a unit. I was proud to see them make a unanimous decision.

"It smells like sewage again," my wife said.

I turned my nose to the air. I hadn't noticed it, but she was right. She was always right. We were having plumbing problems. The ground was saturated with rainwater, making our sinks and toilets drain slowly.

"I'll take care of it," I said with the confidence of a man who doesn't understand the problem. I followed the smell around the house, sniffing the bathrooms, and traced it to the front door.

I followed the smell out into the yard. There was a hole in the ground over our septic tank that hadn't been there before. Septic repairs would be expensive, and I was bleeding our savings on beer and liquor. I'd started buying store brand cereal for the kids, taking it out of the package as soon as I put it in the cupboard so they wouldn't notice. They chewed contemplatively, like they could tell something was different, but they never said anything. They were good kids.

I walked to the edge of the hole, testing the ground with my toes. The smell was worse. A cluster of sewer flies hovered a few feet off the ground. They landed on my nose and ears. I hated to think where they had just been. The septic system was a mystery to me, a terrible-smelling miracle of modern life. When we had to hire people to work on it, I would hide away in the back room as they dragged hoses across the yard. The way they pumped our stinking waste into the tank of a large truck was undignified. I imagined the hangover sludge that leaked out of me every morning being driven across town, on its way to who knows where. The normal people on their commutes had no idea of the filth sloshing alongside them in traffic.

I tried looking into the hole, but all I could see was that it was black and wet, an open wound in the ground. I knew we'd have to put the repairs on credit. Add another line to the ledger. The credit card companies kept sending us offers in the mail and I kept taking them. I'd have to reckon with it someday, but today wasn't the day.

"No problem," I told my wife. "Well, a little problem. A hole. Lots of flies. We'll get someone over to deal with it."

My wife smiled. She trusted me to handle it, which amazed and humbled me. Her eyes, brown and green, caught the fluorescent orange of the cheese powder she was stirring into the macaroni. There were so many colors it made me want to cry. What did I do to deserve this life? I opened another beer.

I spotted a small patch of sewer flies on the living room wall. They must have slipped in when I'd opened the door. Sewer flies live in the worst, wettest, most putrid places.

I wanted to get a can of insecticide, but I thought of my beautiful family and decided against it. Who knew what was in that stuff. I didn't want to be responsible for some major health problem they might have in the future. So I started collecting the flies.

Sewer flies are docile, not like regular houseflies that have developed a tightly honed ability to escape the human hand. Sewer flies must not even understand the threat of a flyswatter, or a rolled-up newspaper, because they generally let you swat them without a fight. One day you'll see one or two, and the next day the whole bathroom is full of them. A sure sign that you've got a leaky pipe somewhere, that they've found a dank spot to reproduce.

I was gentle with them. Their life cycle must be short, I figured. A few days, maybe. Who was I to shorten an already abbreviated life? I knew I could be inconsiderate, not thinking about the experiences of others. I was self-absorbed. I was suffering but I thought no one else was. In trying to be better, when I could, I sometimes found myself showing too much care toward things that didn't deserve it.

The sewer flies sat on the palm of my hand like they had nowhere else they'd rather be. I checked the white wall for black spots. I finished off a beer and left the empty can on the end table by the couch, where I knew I would forget about it and my wife would have to pick it up eventually. But first she'd give me a couple days to notice before finally resigning herself to the fact that I rarely noticed anything.

"You guys want to see something?" I asked the kids.

The kids yelled excitedly, abandoning their macaroni and cheese. I held out my open palm. The sewer flies milled around a little bit, but they didn't take off. "These guys live in our poops," I said. "Isn't that crazy, that we just flush it away, but that's, like, their whole world?"

The kids' faces scrunched up in disgust. Maybe I had been too vigorous about their toilet training. It was a difficult balance to strike, stressing the need for cleanliness without veering too far and giving them hang-ups about their bodily functions.

"Come eat your dinner," my wife said to the kids. "Take those outside, or kill them, whatever." She put her hand on my shoulder and turned me toward the door.

I took a beer and went to sit on the front porch. The smell of sewage was strong, but I found it comforting knowing the flies in my hand would recognize it as home. "Okay guys," I said to my open palm. The sewer flies sat mostly still, fluttering their wings tentatively but not taking flight. "I'm going to have to close up this hole, because it's a hazard, so you should go enjoy this short life while you can." The flies stayed on my palm. They weren't getting it. I drained the beer and wanted another, but when I stood up to go inside the flies buzzed angrily. They hovered then landed in a frenzy, making frantic patterns on my hand each time they landed. They marched around and arranged themselves into shapes that looked like letters. "Are you trying to tell me something?" I asked. They ran up and down my forearm, tracing the veins in my wrist. They circled around my knuckles. They stood at the tips of my fingernails and extended their little legs, like they were praying, or waiting for lightning to strike. I sat back down. I never know what's good for me. My body was deteriorating. I was drunk enough to be sad about the state of my life. And I wanted another beer.

"Tell me what you want," I said to the flies.

They lined up in the creases on my palm. They fluttered their wings, making it feel like my hand was in a tiny breeze. It felt good, and it made me feel better about myself. They really seemed like they wanted to know me, to help me. I was ready, I guess, to give up.

I never try to interpret symbols or poetry, but I could tell the flies wanted me to quit drinking. They cared about me. I held my palm up to my face to get a better view of them. "I love you guys," I said, weepy, because the sun was going down and that kind of thing reminds me of my own mortality. I threw my empty beer can behind the hedges against the house.

The kids were done with their macaroni and cheese. They sat on our dog-stained couch with their legs crossed under them, playing games on tiny screens. My wife was cleaning the kitchen, and I started to help, one hand gathering up plates and cups I'd used throughout the day but hadn't made it to the sink, the other hand cupping the sewer flies gently.

"Why are you holding your hand like that?" my wife asked. She was perceptive. I didn't want to keep anything from her. She was the only person who didn't make me feel bad about myself, even when I deserved it.

"These flies have something to teach me," I said. "I tried letting them go, but they don't want to go anywhere. They want me to stop drinking."

"I told you that," my wife said. "You're confusing me with the sewer flies."

"You both told me. You and the sewer flies. Working in concert. This is a good thing. I'm giving it up," I said.

My wife smiled, but it wasn't a happy smile. She'd heard me say the same thing plenty of times. When I couldn't get off the floor of the bathroom, or when I'd forgotten something important and gotten drunk instead of showing up to whatever it was. It was a sad smile, which is the worst kind of smile.

The sewer flies must have sensed this. They buzzed against my palm and I knew they wanted me to put my hand around her waist. I grabbed her tight and kissed her on the cheek. The sewer flies buzzed at me to ease off a little.

"We'll see," she said, which was even sadder than the sad smile.

The sewer flies told me to empty the rest of the beer down the sink, where my wife had just finished washing dishes, so I did, can after can, resisting the urge to lift each to my mouth and take a drink. They moved around to the back of my hand when they needed to, and when it was safe they nestled back in the hollow of my palm. Their little wings cooled my skin, evaporating the sweat that the humidity normally kept damp. The flies watched happily as the foamy liquid swirled down the drain.

I hoped this was different than all the other times I'd tried to quit drinking, but I had no confidence that I'd be able to change, as desperately as I wanted to. I held my hand close to my chest, hoping the sewer flies could feel the warmth and rhythm of my heart, that they could sense my appreciation.

I'd started to sober up by the time we put the kids to bed. I read them a book for the first time in a while. They watched the sewer flies migrate across my skin as I turned the pages, giggling and pointing, more interested in their movements than the content of the book. It wasn't a very good book. After a few pages I closed it and we watched the flies walk around on my hand, flutter their wings, lick their little front legs clean.

When I crawled into bed beside my wife, my head was already hurting from withdrawals. I knew I'd be shaking before morning. The sewer flies told me to put my arm around her. My wife laced her fingers into mine. The sewer flies crawled from my hand to hers and back again. I thought she would pull away, but she pressed her body into me. Before dawn I'd start puking. I'd be sweating and miserable. I didn't sleep much as I waited, staring at the back of my wife's head. The sewer flies rested on my knuckles, buzzing when I got a little afraid. They would help me through it. They were hatched in sludge, and they knew what it was like to emerge, reborn, to the surface of the toilet water.

THE OTHER
SHANE HINTON

What's up with that new leaf blower?" I asked my neighbor on the afternoon of St. Patrick's Day. I put on a smile and nodded along as he told me the details: its horsepower, its decibel output, its fuel consumption. "Great, great," I said. "That's all super interesting." I was trying to cultivate an attitude of curiosity rather than malice.

"It's capable of uprooting small trees," he said. "I mean, like really small trees. Saplings. Sprouts, maybe is more like it. Still, trees." He raised his eyebrows and lit a cigarette, tilted his head back to blow smoke at a sky the color of purpled meat.

My neighbor bent over the bed of his pickup and pulled out a silver can of beer, ice chips dripping down its side, just like in commercials and in my recurring dreams. I had quit drinking a few months prior and the smell of beer still rattled me. He held out the can to me and I shook my head.

"I can't," I said, but my hand had started reaching out instinctively, a twitch toward oblivion.

He laughed and pushed the can closer. "Just one," he said. "In honor of the holiday."

"I'm Polish," I said. I had forgotten to wear green.

"HAVE YOU BEEN TALKING TO THE NEIGHBORS?" I ASKED MY wife at dinner.

She shrugged. "Define talking."

"Sharing important information. Having emotional or spiritual experiences," I tried.

She thought about it for a moment. "They said we should trim our trees."

I looked out the window at the tall white privacy fence the neighbors had installed. Our infected citrus tree had sent a limb or two over the property line. The ground around its trunk was littered with half-developed fruits that had been gnawed by rodents. Many of our neighbors walked together in the evenings. Their yards were nicely edged. The outsides of their homes presented calm, order, structure. That night we heard our next-door neighbors up late, yelling things at each other that sounded fun for a while and then not very fun at all.

THE UNIVERSITY WHERE I WORKED HAD ONCE BEEN A hotel. Classrooms and faculty offices were housed in old suites with fireplaces covered by sheet metal. The water fountain outside my office leaked gently onto the carpet, spreading a dark stain that periodically dried and reformed.

It was the midpoint of the semester and it seemed important to carry the momentum. I put funny images in my slide show presentations on punctuation. I drank too much black coffee, swishing it around in my mouth, even though my dentist told me to stop doing that, to rinse with water after each cup. I licked my yellowing teeth.

The students exhaled loudly when I walked in and set down my bag. I figured they were ashamed of their behavior the previous night. St. Patrick's Day was popular among the student body. The students with any Irish heritage at all, a distant relative their grandparents had once mentioned or a couple percentage points on a DNA profile, felt emboldened. But the students looked rested, not hungover.

I turned on the projector. They crossed their arms. They were silent. I stopped what I was doing and held my palms up to let them know I was picking up on the awkwardness in the room.

"We know what you did," they said.

"I've done many things I wouldn't want to share with you," I said, "but I'm not sure which of these you're referring to."

They held up their phones. On the screens were mugshots of a man that looked a lot like me. The same poor beard shape, the same lazy hairstyle, the same bloated look in the cheeks that caused the eyes to appear smaller, the same partial smile I always put on for pictures because my front tooth is chipped. Shane Hinton, the caption said. Arrested March 17. St. Patrick's Day.

"Domestic violence," they said. "We figured class would be canceled. We made plans to go to that museum our parents are always guilting us into visiting. Our parents were going to be so happy."

That got my heart going. I could feel the vein in my neck pulsing, straining against itself. "It's always a good day to go to that museum," I said. "You don't need an excuse. Let me see that."

They pulled back their phones. "We can't believe the university would hire somebody like you. It's proof of all the things we thought might be true about the world but hoped were not."

I remembered dinner the night before. Salad with baked chicken breasts, very calorie-conscious. The dog nosing open our bedroom door in the night, the jangle of her collar in the hallway. Was it possible that somewhere in the middle of all that I'd slipped out, gotten drunk, beaten someone, gotten arrested?

I lectured about commas, which was my least favorite part of the curriculum, but I knew it was important for them, as young people, to learn to pause between thoughts, to demonstrate pensiveness on the page. The students stared at their laptop screens and tapped at their phones. They didn't say "thank you" the way they often did at the end of class, which was okay because it always made me feel like I had to say "thank you" back, even though most days I didn't feel very thankful at the end of class.

As soon as the last student left I opened my laptop and pulled up the arrest record. It wasn't me. He had a different middle name, a different date of birth. There was no way it could be me, I told myself, tracing the shape of my nose with the tip of my finger, comparing it to his.

I drafted a department-wide email:

"To Whom it May Concern."

I stopped. That was wrong. Too formal. Exactly the kind of voice a domestic abuser would put on. I held down the backspace key.

"Folks," I started again.

Better. Non-threatening. I knew my colleagues thought of me as a redneck because I'd grown up on a strawberry farm.

"It may have been brought to your attention that someone sharing my first and last name—but not my middle name! not my birthdate!—was arrested last night on a charge of domestic violence. I want to assure you that any violence in my past was of the merciful variety, such as when my dogs all-but-killed a squirrel in the yard and I had to sever its head with the blade of a shovel, or when we ran over a rattlesnake in our minivan and I backed up to hit it a couple more times before driving on.

"I spent this St. Patrick's Day at home, sleeping poorly because the neighbors were so loud. Plus, and I didn't want to mention this, I've been sober a few months now. I hesitate to bring this up with you, not from embarrassment, exactly, but more from the sense that one ought to keep certain things to oneself, such as descriptions of dreams, current spread and loss of body hair, and so on.

"I am sure by this point you've taken a moment to locate the arrest record on your own, and I won't link to it here, because I don't want to seem too desperate to prove my innocence, and why should I be? Is it the responsibility of the innocent to advocate for themselves? I encourage you all, if you can't accept my declarations, to do your own research and compare my faculty photo from the department website with the level of puffiness in this other Shane Hinton's face, the redness of his nose, the pattern of his beard, which, yes, I admit is similar to mine in many ways, and, sure, do I now regret having my faculty photo taken during an ill-advised period of beard growth? Yes, of course I do. If I'd known this other Shane Hinton was out there, growing a similarly bad beard, continuing to drink, getting ready to become domestically violent, I would have shaved my beard before the start-of-semester faculty reception where they take those photos. Of course I would have. It was the end of summer. I was trying things out. I shaved it just a few days after that picture was taken. I did not commit to the look."

As I passed my colleagues on the way to the parking lot, they took their phones out of their pockets and looked down, brows furrowed like they were doing something important, but when I leaned over to look their screens were black.

THE UNIVERSITY WAS CLOSE TO THE PORT AND I HEADED there to buy seafood like I usually did when my day had gone poorly, when students had accused me of unfair grading practices or I'd procrastinated past an important deadline. The delicate tissue of shrimp or scallops heating up in the passenger seat gave me a reason to hurry home, the levels of bacteria inside them steadily rising, the flesh liquefying imperceptibly.

A man in a wide-brimmed hat leaned back in a folding chair under a beach umbrella by the entrance to the docks. Beside him, a hand-painted sign read: BLUE CRABS, CARRION EATERS, JANITORS OF THE SEA. He rested his feet on a cooler and poked a pair of tongs into a plastic tub that brimmed with crabs trying to escape. When I got out of my car, he took off his sunglasses, raised the brim of his hat and smiled. It was the other Shane Hinton. I recognized him immediately from his mugshot. I looked over my shoulder, afraid people might think we were friends, or brothers. No one else was around.

"How did you get a fresh catch already?" I asked. "Aren't you supposed to be in jail?"

"The tide waits for no man," he said. "You're that other Shane Hinton. I recognize you from your faculty photo. Need some crabs?"

My hands started to sweat. "I had a bad day," I said.

"Boy, so did I," he said. "The cops took my shoelaces. Told me I was a suicide risk. I told them I'd never been less at risk of suicide in my life. It was life-affirming, being this low. I was seeing things from a new angle. Suicide? Not in a moment of enlightenment like this. Still," he gestured at his tennis shoes, laceless, their sides flopping away from each other.

"I was thinking of putting together a boil," I said, "but I don't really know what all goes into it." I'd always heard that a good boil was varied yet consistent. The meal needed to tell a story that moved from protein into root vegetable. Its salt levels needed to mimic the salinity of the ocean.

The other Shane Hinton started poking metal tongs into the plastic tub. "Oh yeah, I can help you with that." He picked up one crab and turned it over in the sunlight, studying it. Its claws grabbed at the tongs, pinching and releasing, moving up and down, trying to find something to hurt. "You'll need a couple dozen of these guys at least," he said. "I say 'guys' only informally, by the way. There are plenty of females in here. Their bellies tell the story. Look for the shapes of famous statuary. Some people like to be acquainted with the sex of their dinners. It feels virile, I guess, if you're struggling with that sort of thing. The meat of opposing sexes mixing within you. Very symbolic."

The other Shane Hinton opened a paper grocery bag and dropped in the crab. He reached into the tub and pulled out two more. One crab wriggled in the grip of the tongs. The other had clamped its claws onto one of the first crab's thin legs, spinning freely on the appendage.

"Can their legs handle that?"

He frowned. "No," he said. "They're turning on each other." He shook the tongs and the leg snapped off, sending the one crab back into the plastic tub, the mass writhing at the disturbance. The crab with the missing leg moved more slowly, its claws closing on the air. "This one is going to die, and when he dies he'll release a toxin that will kill any others close by. Pretty soon you've got a chain reaction on your hands. You haven't smelled anything until you've smelled a good crab die-off." He dropped the wounded crab into the grass at our feet. It wandered around in circles, probably missing the pull of the waves, probably listening for the muffled sounds of outboard motors. The other Shane Hinton lifted a laceless shoe and stepped down hard on its back. It crunched audibly. Its legs went still.

"What will eat it now?" I asked.

"You know, birds, probably," the other Shane Hinton said. He filled the bag until the pile of crabs inside bulged against the brown paper, then handed it to me. "I'll come by around eight. Show you how to put this thing together." He reached into the scarred plastic cooler, pulling a can of beer from the ice water. "You ready to fall off the wagon yet?" He held the lid of the cooler open and nodded toward the silver cans bobbing gently under the surface. Crabs scraped against the paper bag, brushing against my arms.

"Why are you doing this to me?"

"I think we're doing this to each other," he said.

WHEN I GOT HOME THE NEIGHBOR WAS BLOWING OFF HIS driveway. It smelled like exhaust and dry dirt. "Hey, sicko," he said, shutting down the leaf blower. "Saw your arrest record. Why do you think I'm always out here uprooting small trees? You think I have something against small trees? Not at all. I like them. I like the way their stalks are capable of growing into trunks you can't even fit your arms around. Buddy, I'm out here to keep an eye on things." Around our feet lay several small plants, recently upturned, their leaves against the pavement, their thin white roots reaching toward the sky. The neighbor pulled the starter and cranked up his leaf blower, sending the small plants out into the middle of the street. A cloud of dust rose around my legs and scraped the inside of my throat.

My wife sat at the kitchen counter drinking a glass of red wine. Little pieces of cork floated on the surface. Before I quit drinking, I used to fish them out for her with the tip of my finger, then lick my fingers clean. I salivated at the memory of the taste. She was highlighting an entire page of the book open in front of her. "Aren't you supposed to be in jail?" she asked.

"I was here last night," I said. "Remember? I read while you worked on your research? I said that inconsiderate thing about the noise of your typing? I apologized almost immediately, exhibiting great humility? I slept next to you? I only snored a little?"

She narrowed her eyes. "Yeah, I guess that sounds familiar." She was used to believing the bad things she heard about me.

"Want me to get the cork out for you?" I asked, pointing at her glass. She slid it closer to herself and kept working.

I tried a breathing exercise I had learned about. In, two, three, four. Out, two, three, four. Navy SEALs used this same exercise, according to a commenter on the article I'd read. They lay in saltwater, letting waves lap at their nostrils, breathing like this for hours, ignoring the way the skin on their fingers and toes wrinkled up like corpse flesh.

There would almost certainly be online petitions calling for my firing by now. I would be expected to lower my head and move on, get another job in a field that doesn't do stringent background checks. Have some dignity, I told myself, breathing in through my nose and out through my mouth. Don't go down thrashing, causing a ruckus. The little pieces of cork bobbed on the surface of my wife's drink.

There was a knock at the side door. The other Shane Hinton was there, next to the herb planter I hadn't tended in months. The chives were almost up to his head, their white flowers growing in round bulbs. The other Shane Hinton smiled with half his mouth. Across the street, the neighbor exhaled a puff of smoke and stared.

"You found it," I said.

"I followed my nose," the other Shane Hinton said, tapping his red nose. I let him in and he sat at the counter next to my wife, who was working on another page, pink highlighter ink bleeding through the paper.

"Who did you beat on?" I asked.

"The people closest to me," the other Shane Hinton said. He didn't give the half-smile now. His puffy cheeks trembled a little. "I didn't want to beat on them." He looked down at his hands, turning them over, flexing his knuckles. He curled his fingers in, looked at his nails. "I just get stuck in high gear."

"Would you email my colleagues?" I asked. "Maybe we could take a picture together. We could each hold signs with our middle names and birthdates."

"I'm not appearing in any pictures," the other Shane Hinton said, pulling a beer from his bulging pants pocket. "Let's get this boil going." The paper bag of crabs jostled on the counter, like they knew what was coming. I'd already pulled out the extra-tall pot my wife had gotten me for Christmas, the one meant especially for the kind of cooking where you put disparate things together, the kind of cooking that takes up a lot of space.

The other Shane Hinton took a crab out of the bag. It didn't have the same energy it had on the roadside. "Just a few hours out of the sea and they start to forget who they are." He set the crab on the counter and turned it over on its back. "Look at the belly," he said. "What figure from history do you see?"

"Joan of Arc?" I guessed. I didn't see any historical

figures. The lines in its shell seemed purely geometric.

"And you?" the other Shane Hinton asked, turning the crab so my wife could see.

"Julius Caesar," she said, then went back to highlighting.

The other Shane Hinton looked at the underside of the crab for a moment, then nodded. "How do you know so much about crabs?"

My wife shrugged. She took a sip of her wine and drew her highlighter across another line, going slowly, making even and steady marks on the page.

The lid of the extra-tall pot clanked around as the water started to boil. The other Shane Hinton lifted the lid and dropped in the crab.

"Don't you need to kill it first?" I asked. "Like, knife it behind the eyes or something?" I had been taught to dispatch crabs quickly, just before cooking them.

"Wouldn't matter," the other Shane Hinton said. "Its nervous system isn't centralized. You can't apply what you know about yourself to crabs. It's not a clean comparison."

AFTER DINNER I WAS OVERFULL. MY STOMACH PRESSED against the edge of the table. My hands smelled like low tide. The crabs hadn't tasted very fresh even though I'd watched them trying to escape the boiling water. Their emptied-out shells were scattered in front of us. The other Shane Hinton picked his teeth. He pulled another beer out of his pants pocket. It couldn't have been cold anymore. I studied the sides of his legs, trying to gauge how many cans he might still have in there.

My wife poured more wine into her glass. Tiny pieces of cork had dried near the rim.

"Give me a ride home?" he asked. I didn't want to take him back to the people he was closest to, but he had started to arch his back and eye the couch. I didn't want to think about what the neighbor would say if the other Shane Hinton was still there the next morning, when the neighborhood kids were getting on the buses to head to school.

It was humid enough outside to fog the windows of my car even with the air conditioner on. Across the street, a crane from the ongoing construction was outlined against a red moon. "We need to watch our sodium intake," the other Shane Hinton said, toeing a pile of hamburger wrappers on the floorboard.

I shrugged. My doctor had told me my blood vessels were constricted. Whenever there were pains in my heart I took them as the product of a life poorly lived.

I drove through the suburbs, past the houses of my childhood friends. "Here's where we had our first kiss," I said. "We laughed and accidentally drooled into her mouth."

"Sure," the other Shane Hinton said. "I remember that. It was late, right? We shouldn't have been out that late."

"It was safer back then," I said. "And we had skateboards to swing at people if we needed to." We passed strip malls and vacant lots. "There's where we fell off the skateboard and got that chunk of rock stuck in our knee. It still hurts when we're on an airplane."

"Must be the air pressure," the other Shane Hinton said. "Our bodies weren't made to be pressurized and de-pressurized like that. Stop here." He pointed to the back of a restaurant. "Remember when Jeff worked here and we'd smoke cigarettes with him on his break? Remember how he told us he'd put his feet in the soup, so to never order the soup?"

I could almost smell the metallic tomato soup Jeff used to ladle out to old women at brunch. "Jeff died," I said. "Single-car accident."

"A tragedy," the other Shane Hinton said. "His fiancé planted a tree over his ashes."

"But it died, too," I said. A lemon tree, chosen for its metaphorical significance rather than its longevity.

We drove on, out of the suburbs. The streetlights grew farther apart and then disappeared entirely. We rolled our windows down.

"We used to be so happy to just drive around," the other Shane Hinton said.

"Gas was cheaper."

"The people I'm closest to said I can't come back until I'm better, but I don't think I can get any better. I think I've reached the peak of my personal development." He held his hand out the window and let the passing air lift it, then let it drop. "I'm on the downslope."

I knew what he meant. Once inertia set in it was easy to get bumped along by the current.

"Here it is," he said, directing me to a trailer by a small green pond. A sign read ALLIGATORS PRESENT - NO SWIMMING. The trailer was brown and white with a single light over the front door. Shapes moved behind the curtain, back and forth. Pacing.

"You're going to get me fired," I said.

The other Shane Hinton wiped a fake tear from his eye. "That job is no good for you anyway."

"My students think I'm going to beat on them."

"Oh come on," he said. "Look at these hands. Do you really think these hands could strangle the people I'm closest to?" He held up his hands and I tried to guess how wide they could spread, if they could wrap around the neck of an adult, a child.

I suddenly became aware that my headlights were shining directly on the windows of the trailer. I imagined what it was like behind those windows, the headlights making shadows fall at angles the sunlight never could.

"I don't know," I said. "They just seem like hands to me."

TO SPILL IT
OR GIVE IT AWAY

We had been beset by several plagues, including moths in our closets that ate my denim jacket, a stomach illness that had us all shitting ourselves for six nights straight, and a flood from the underside of our washing machine that spilled soapy water over our shoes so that we walked around squishing out soap bubbles everywhere we went. It was the grasshoppers, though, that broke us. They swarmed over the peach tree my wife had given me on the first Father's Day after our kids were born. I don't know much about insects, but anyone could see these grasshoppers were just hatched and they were hungry. They perched on top of the ripening fruit, their serrated legs jutting toward the sky, and ate the tiny peaches down to the pits.

I stood in the yard looking at those wrinkled little pits. I had wanted to make peach cobbler, which I had promised to my kids. They didn't really like peach cobbler, but I wasn't sure what else to make out of peaches. I don't like things that are soft and fleshy. The kids stood behind me on the sidewalk. I don't know how many there were or what their names were. Did I love them? Of course I did. But memory is imperfect.

"Daddy," they said. "Did those bugs eat your peaches?"

I've never been prone to violence, or any good at it, but I couldn't bear the looks on their little faces as they realized for the first time that a planted seed might not grow. There would only be so many peach seasons before they headed off to college and didn't want to eat a cobbler their dad made. The way I saw it, those grasshoppers were eating up my kids' childhoods. I felt a need for vengeance.

The insects crawled over the sidewalk and I started stomping them with my bare feet. It wasn't a very well thought out plan. There were thousands of them, crawling over each other, moving through the grass. I would never be able to eradicate the threat. But I couldn't help myself. The kids joined in and soon there were green grasshopper guts spilled all over the sidewalk, over our toes and the sides of our feet. It didn't smell like anything, really, other than the freshly cut grass that had been their spawning grounds, but I imagined that it smelled. I imagine a lot of things.

My wife opened the screen door and all of our children, hundreds of them it seemed, all exactly the same age and with the same hairstyle, swarmed around her calves, clinging to the hem of her yellow summer dress.

"I made lemonade," she said, and the kids cheered, because lemonade was one of the few sugary drinks we allowed them to have, because we were trying to prevent them from developing an addiction to sweets, because we wanted their organs to function cleanly so they would live long, happy lives and learn to love the same things that gave us joy. My wife set a tray of glasses down. The kids slurped at them and abandoned the empty glasses all over the yard. Grasshoppers crawled into the glasses, dipping their antennae into the liquid. My wife hugged me, pressing her head into my chest as the kids spun circles in the yard, crushing insects between their toes.

Of course, this is just a story. None of that really happened. I want to save you, to save myself, but each sentence feels further from the truth.

WHEN I WAS NINE, I FOUND A COW UP TO ITS NECK IN quicksand in the middle of the creek that ran through our farm. She lowered her head and drank from the muddy water. I sat behind the house, listening to the grinding of a tractor engine as the rancher tried to pull her out. The engine whined. The cow screamed. After a while, the engine shut off and the pasture was silent. A few minutes later a gunshot rang across the palmettos, across ditches of decomposing muck. I don't remember any sounds after that.

MY FAVORITE ANIMAL IS THE GENTLE MANATEE. AT THE aquarium where I took my kids to see the oldest one living in captivity, they told us sailors used to mistake them for mermaids. My daughters pressed their faces against the side of the tank. My son read the placard beneath the manatee skeleton mounted on the wall behind us. Manatees have the same hand bones as humans, but they're covered over with rubbery gray skin. They can only touch in a general way, but the bones are there, waiting for some evolutionary need, some miracle of time and breeding, to be uncovered.

The aquarium staff had trained the manatee to do tricks for lettuce. He climbed on the deck of the pool where he lived his restricted little life and took the leaves from his keeper's hand. My daughters clapped. My son looked up at the sun coming through the skylight.

A month after our visit someone left a panel loose in his tank, and the manatee wedged himself in among the pump machinery and drowned. It takes a manatee a long time to drown. The live camera feed from his tank showed his large round tail sticking out of the machinery, flipping ever more slowly, unable to propel him backward. They took down the camera feed after he died.

Some other manatee is the oldest living manatee in captivity now.

DO NOT CUT A BABY'S FINGERNAILS.

Do not spin a chair on one leg.

Bite the head from the first butterfly of spring.

You must not waste salt. You must not spill it or give it away.

You invite tragedy by opening an umbrella indoors. Depend on the house, on its walls and roof, for protection.

Stand in the first rainfall in May.

Do not eat the point of a piece of pie first.

If you do spill salt, throw a pinch over your left shoulder. Waste just a little more of what has been wasted, but purposefully, ceremonially.

I hate it when the kids spill salt. I walk around throwing it over my shoulder, just in case they've spilled some and I missed it. The floor of our kitchen is littered with tiny granules. I don't want to sweep them up. If I gather them in the dust pan, then into a garbage bag, is that a further waste? What will happen if I take that garbage bag out to the street, if it gets hauled away to the dump, the salt crystals inside having flavored nothing, having preserved nothing? I search books for references, but they only go so far. There is no ambiguity in their pronouncements.

You must not waste salt.

You must not spill it or give it away.

MY KIDS SMASHED GRASSHOPPERS UNTIL THEIR FACES were red and dripping with sweat. They coated the grass with a sticky green residue. We couldn't bring the peaches back, but we had our revenge.

"Daddy," my kids said, "why is it that some peaches live so long on the branch and some peaches die as blossoms in the freeze? Why does God send the grasshoppers to eat the fruit of our trees when he knows we are looking forward to peach cobbler? Why did the hurricane almost blow our peach tree over and why did the tree stay alive, crooked, leaning out over our chain link fence?"

I sat down on the sticky grass to be eye level with them. I put my face next to theirs so we could each feel the other's breath. "The hurricane was strong enough to blow the tree over, but not strong enough to kill it," I said. "Remember how we huddled together in the closet, waiting for the wind to pass?"

The kids nodded. They had been scared. The portable radio we'd brought into the closet blared tornado warnings. The eye of the storm passed within a few miles of our house.

I felt myself shifting into parable. "The wind of the storm tried to tear the tree down because it wanted us to think about the peaches, but not be able to eat them. The wind is always hungry for our disappointment. It siphons our body heat and whisks away good smells."

The kids pressed their heads against my shoulder and started crying a little bit into my shirt. They didn't like being reminded of the wind. A little breeze rose up to dry the tears from their cheeks and they flinched.

"It's okay," I said. "You don't have to be afraid of this wind. Remember how we build houses to protect ourselves from it?" I lifted their chins to meet my eyes. Though they were scared, they looked at me with determination. "Always remember, though the wind might try to kill us, the peach tree survived, and though the grasshoppers ate the fruit from our tree, that fruit grew and flourished, even if it didn't make it to our table in the form of the cobbler we had hoped for."

The kids cast their eyes at the crooked trunk of the peach tree. It would never be sturdy enough for them to climb, because it had been so damaged by the wind, and because its roots were partially exposed, forced to grow in new directions. I stood and we walked around the yard, cataloguing the things that were dead and the things that were still living. The grasshoppers were dead. There was no arguing that. The branches from the stunted palm tree in the corner of the yard were dead. The catkins that fell from the oak tree were dead, having fulfilled their purpose in releasing pollen.

We were alive. Our dog was alive. The frogs that lived in our pool were alive.

The wind, the kids tried to argue, was alive, but the wind, I explained, was neither alive nor dead. It existed in a state of being that was not recognizable to us, whose experience of the world is framed by birth and death. The wind would continue blowing over peach trees and blowing the roofs off barns and blowing ships sideways until they took on water and capsized long after we were dead.

The wind, I tried to make them see, didn't care where it blew. The problem was that we were in the way.

ONE NIGHT I FOUND A DEER AT THE END OF OUR DRIVEWAY. Its hind legs had been crippled by a passing car. It tried to run away and tangled itself in a barbed wire fence.

I rested the barrel of a rifle on the hood of the car and shot it once through the neck. It jerked upward, toward the tops of the young oak trees, then it was still.

Can we, in dying, gesture beyond our capacity for suffering?

A bag of fried fish sat next to me on the seat, growing soggy. When I ate it, the damp batter sloughed off to reveal silver scales that at one time had reflected the patterns of the waves, a sky clear and clouded in turn. I can still hear the deer crying.

WE SAW THE CARCASS OF THE ENDANGERED FLORIDA panther on the side of the road. I stopped the minivan and dragged the kids out onto the muddy shoulder to witness the animal's sacrifice. We don't often see the Florida panther, because there are so few left their extinction is inevitable. They hide in the woods of the Everglades, only occasionally venturing into a suburb to eat from the trash, to sunbathe on a cinderblock wall.

We stood around the carcass, clearly already a few days dead, its bones sticking through its brown fur, and realized it was a deer. Deer are not endangered. They are everywhere.

My kids were disappointed.

Back in the minivan, our wheels spun in the mud. We sank deeper and deeper until it was clear we were stuck.

I shoved sticks and rocks from the side of the road under the tires, trying to gain traction, but the minivan wouldn't move. I unloaded the kids and they leaned against fenceposts in the shade of a low oak tree.

After some time a truck slowed beside us on the road and offered to help. A man with a white African parrot on his shoulder told us that his son had just died, that he'd inherited the parrot, which he expected to outlive him. He retrieved a tow rope from the toolbox in the bed of his truck, slowly, because he was old and obese. He struggled to navigate the lumpy ground. I attached the rope to the man's trailer hitch and dug in the mud so I could tie it to the axle of our minivan.

"Lord, please let this young man attach this rope to his vehicle so that we may retrieve it from the side of this road without further damage. Lord, please give this young man the strength to dig into the mud, to create a space for his hands and arms to reach under this minivan. Guide his fingers so that they may knot this rope tight and sure around his axle, so that we may pull this vehicle out from the mud and get this family on the road."

The prayers worked. When the van was free, the man shook my muddy hand and sent us on our way. The parrot never spoke a word.

Later that night while hosing mud off the minivan, I found a bird carcass mangled in the grill. It had disintegrated on impact. I couldn't even tell what color its feathers had originally been, because they were brown with dried blood.

NEVER BEGIN A SENTENCE WITH "AND" OR "BUT."

Never end a sentence with a preposition.

And never split an infinitive.

A written thing is a powerful thing.

Stories tell of tentacled monsters waiting just under the surfaces of rivers and lakes. They warn children away from bodies of water to keep them from drowning.

The winter I met my wife, temperatures stayed below freezing for eleven days. To protect their crops, strawberry farmers pumped water onto the fields so that the ice kept the strawberries at a safe thirty-two degrees. I walked through the fields. My shoes crunched through the thin layer of ice and down into mud.

After the fourth day, the aquifer was so drained by the farmers all over town, in the place where my parents and grandparents made a living growing a summer fruit in the winter, hundreds of sinkholes spread across the county. We had three on our farm. One opened up under the pond my grandfather dug. I stood near the edge of the hole and watched the dirt crumble down, listened as it splashed far below the surface. It sucked the pond dry.

There was a largemouth bass in the pond that I had caught and released hundreds of times over the years, identifiable by the scars in his lip where hooks had been set and removed. He lived in the tangled branches of a tree blown into the pond by a hurricane. He disappeared into the sinkhole along with everything else.

There's still a ragged depression where the sinkhole changed the shoreline of the pond. I don't walk near it.

SHOW ME THE STRAIGHT WAY THROUGH TO THE CLIMAX, the denouement, the acknowledgments, the back cover.

Put these words on my heart.

Teach them to my children.

Write them on the doorframe of my house.

Tattoo them on the bony parts of my body, where there is no muscle.

Scream them.

Start so close to the action you can feel it brush past your calves, like a snake in a muddy river.

Find a way to love your characters before you have time to hate them.

Discover who they are by showing how they shuffle their feet, the shapes of their scars, the way their tongues slip out to wet their lips.

Do not trust anyone who would cross out your words and replace them. Carefully erase the marks they make on your pages and restore your text to its original state.

The rough draft is the closest we ever come to the divine.

If I keep trying to tell you this story, there will come a time when the events and the telling of them overlap, one atop the other, and you will be there with me, and the language won't matter anymore.

OUR NEIGHBOR SHOWED UP WITH A CHAINSAW AND OUR kids gathered around to see how it worked. He was always bringing out some new piece of lawn care equipment. It was impressive, more so because I knew nothing about lawn care, or equipment.

"I oiled the chain," he said, showing me the blade.

I nodded, pretending to assess his work. "That's a finely oiled chain," I said. "Looks like it could cut anything that might need cutting."

We stood around the peach tree. The kids plucked the bare pits hanging from the branches and tossed them to the ground. The trunk of the peach tree angled out and barely cleared the top of the fence. Branches on the low side brushed against the ground. The grasshoppers didn't have to jump far to get to the most productive parts of the tree. Most of them didn't even jump. They just climbed.

Our neighbor lit a cigarette and the kids wrinkled their noses. He was in the middle of a divorce. It had gotten ugly. Things started showing up by the curb that still looked useful: potted plants, floor lamps, wicker chairs. I wanted to bring the detritus in, give it a new home, but my wife reminded me we didn't have any more room. Our house was already full. Forgotten clothes and electronics spilled out of our closets.

The neighbor flicked his cigarette out into the yard. The grass was dry. I looked to see where it landed, watched the smoke rise lazily from the tip. He lifted the chainsaw and smiled, spit foaming at the corner of his mouth. The kids backed away, though I had never taught them to be afraid of chainsaws. I didn't want them to be scared of useful things. He pulled the cord, the engine caught, and his arms vibrated. The kids' eyes were wide. My wife looked out through the kitchen window, the yellow curtains parted by her long face. I wanted to step back, hold my arms out to shield the kids from the spinning blade, but I forced myself to plant my feet. I didn't want the kids, the neighbor, to see my fear.

"It can cut through any kind of wood," my neighbor yelled over the roar of the chainsaw. He squeezed the trigger and the blade spun. When he wobbled slightly in my direction, just a brief change of trajectory, I involuntarily stepped back. My neighbor smiled.

My neighbor knew a lot about plants. He was always cutting his in just the right way to make them grow new sprigs. His yard was much nicer than ours. He stood next to the crooked trunk of our peach tree, which had once been a thin twig. Our yard had supplied all the vital nutrients to grow it from a sickly little twig engineered in a university laboratory to grow in Florida, where peach trees have not historically thrived, to the mature tree that now stood before us, covered only a few weeks ago in blossoms, covered now in wrinkled brown pits. The grasshoppers seemed to know something was coming. The trunk looked alive with them, wiggling. They didn't know what a chainsaw could do to their little bodies, to the tree that had so recently supplied them with the stringy flesh of young peaches, peaches that never had the chance to ripen.

My neighbor pulled the throttle and leaned forward, put his weight on the saw, and cut clean through the crooked trunk. The tree fell hard against the chain link fence, denting the metal pole at the top, bending it down toward the ground.

"Whoops," my neighbor said, laughing a little as he cut the engine. I laughed too. Our fence was in terrible shape. One little bent pole wasn't going to get me down.

The grasshoppers leapt from the tree. The kids swarmed around the fallen trunk, fascinated to see it on the ground. They tried climbing it, but it turned under their feet. They tumbled off into the grass.

"Want me to cut this up for you?" my neighbor asked, gesturing the saw at the tree, at the pile of kids rolling around in the yard.

I shook my head. I was having a hard enough time thinking about the wound where the trunk used to be, open to the world, to the fungi that fester in the humidity. I knew the old trunk would sit there and dry up against the fence, because I was always neglecting things.

"Fine by me," my neighbor said. He left the yard through the side gate. A week later he was gone, moved back up north with his family. The house went up for sale.

We waited to see who would move in. Every time a car slowed to look at the house, the kids rushed to the window, crowding against each other to see who our new neighbors might be. Their little faces were so beautiful in the sunlight. I couldn't bring myself to tell them it would probably be bought by investors, shuffled around from owner to owner, each person squeezing the thinnest profit from it before passing it along to some other sucker taken in by the dream of home ownership in this mythical place, about which so many stories are told, into which so many diseases are born.

ACKNOWLEDGMENTS

Thank you:

To Ryan Rivas, one of the best friends I've ever had, for his sharp editorial eye and willingness to keep this slow train rolling.

To Nathan Deuel, Asha Dore, Tyler Gillespie, Alex Gurtis, Gloria Muñoz, and Yuly Restrepo, my dear friends and first readers for their time and feedback.

To Mikhail Iossel for organizing the retreat that allowed me time to finish this project.

To Josip Novakovich for his kind words.

To Erica Dawson, for being in the trenches.

Always, to Lidia Yuknavitch and Jeff Parker.

To Mom, Dad, and Melissa for helping me grow up.

To Jess, Further, Vera, and Iris for being in my stories.

ABOUT THE AUTHOR

Shane Hinton is the author of the story collection *Pinkies*, the novel *Radio Dark*, and editor of the anthology *We Can't Help It If We're From Florida*. He teaches writing at the University of Tampa and lives in the winter strawberry capital of the world.

Photo by Iris & Vera Hinton

www.ingramcontent.com/pod-product-compliance
Lightning Source LLC
Chambersburg PA
CBHW030027200726

48283CB00014B/2719